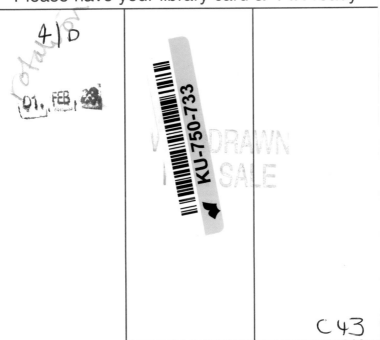

Dear Reader

I'm so grateful to be bringing you another book for the fabulous Mills and Boon® Medical Romances™. I love writing these stories. More than that, I love hearing from readers who ask me when I'm going to write a book featuring the Philippines or India or Barbados. It's humbling, knowing all the many places my books are being read.

THE DOCTOR'S LOST-AND-FOUND HEART takes us to Argentina, one of the most spectacular countries in the world. It also has the most amazingly friendly and resilient people, which is why I chose this setting for my story. It simply seemed like the place Jack and Amanda should be. Of course they're both a little resistant to that. Resistant to each other as well. But Amanda is transformed from a very unanimated woman when she's at home in Texas to someone who's positively hot-blooded the instant she steps foot on Argentine soil. So what's that about? You'll have to read the book to see.

Then there's Jack, a man from nowhere, going no place in particular. He wants to avoid Argentina at all costs, but when duty calls he will always put aside his personal needs and answer. In the case of Argentina, the cost of his call is the highest price he may ever have to pay.

THE DOCTOR'S LOST-AND-FOUND HEART follows Jack Kenner's story—a story begun in NO. 1 DAD IN TEXAS, which preceded this book. And there'll be another story to follow, also set in Argentina, featuring Amanda's brother Ben.

In the meantime, I'm finally joining the social media revolution. So please follow and like me at www.Facebook.com (DianneDrakeAuthor), and jump over to see what I'm tweeting @DianneDrake. Feel free to stop by my website (www.DianneDrake.com) as well, and e-mail me with suggestions for another amazing country in which to set one of my stories. I've just about exhausted my travel supply, so now it's time to start broadening my horizons.

As always, wishing you health and happiness.

DD

Now that her children have left home, **Dianne Drake** is finally finding the time to do some of the things she adores—gardening, cooking, reading, shopping for antiques. Her absolute passion in life, however, is adopting abandoned and abused animals. Right now Dianne and her husband Joel have a little menagerie of three dogs and two cats, but that's always subject to change. A former symphony orchestra member, Dianne now attends the symphony as a spectator several times a month and, when time permits, takes in an occasional football, basketball or hockey game.

THE DOCTOR'S LOST-AND-FOUND HEART

BY
DIANNE DRAKE

First published in Great Britain 2012
by Mills & Boon, an imprint of Harlequin (UK) Limited.
Large Print edition 2013
Harlequin (UK) Limited, Eton House,
18-24 Paradise Road, Richmond, Surrey TW9 1SR

© Dianne Despain 2012

ISBN: 978 0 263 23101 4

Printed and bound in Great Britain
by CPI Antony Rowe, Chippenham, Wiltshire

Recent titles by Dianne Drake:

NO. 1 DAD IN TEXAS
THE RUNAWAY NURSE
FIREFIGHTER WITH A FROZEN HEART
THE DOCTOR'S REASON TO STAY**
FROM BROODING BOSS TO ADORING DAD
THE BABY WHO STOLE THE DOCTOR'S HEART*
CHRISTMAS MIRACLE: A FAMILY*

**New York Hospital Heartthrobs
Mountain Village Hospital

**These books are also available in
eBook format from www.millsandboon.co.uk**

To Doctor Nance,
the ID specialist who saved my life.
You made the diagnosis
when nobody else could find the 'bug'.
Thank you.

CHAPTER ONE

WRAPPED around her pretty little finger. That was how he felt, traipsing around out here in God-forsaken nowhere, with nothing but a backpack full of testing supplies and a sneaking suspicion that there was going to be more to this mission than a couple of days. Way more than a couple of days...

Jack Kenner swatted a mosquito on his neck, flicked it away, then wiped the sweat off his face with the back of his hand. If he'd been smart about this, or had had time to plan, he'd have had his hair buzzed down to a bald cut, because collar-length wavy and summer jungle humidity weren't a good mix. And it was damn humid out here. Unseasonably so for mid-December. He'd have also had time to order adequate testing supplies—he never liked to go unprepared. But when Amanda had called him, told him what was at risk, and that it was urgent… First plane out. What could he say? He was a sucker for a beautiful face and a worthy cause. She certainly had the beautiful face, and a bunch of sick kids was a worthy cause.

Thinking about her brought a smile to *his* face. Amanda Robinson. More than beautiful, actually. Stunning. Exquisite. Wild, black hair when it wasn't all trussed up. Dark skin. Eyes the color of onyx. Exotic in every sense of the word. A real breathtaker who was totally unaware of the power she could hold over a man.

Outside a handful of professional encounters back in Texas, Jack hardly even knew the woman, yet here he was, somewhere in Argentina, because she'd asked. The hell of it was, he didn't do that kind of looking anymore. Kept it strictly off his radar. Except when Amanda walked by him that first time his radar had blipped. For him, though, one or two blips and that was as far as it went. His life was screwed up in every way that counted and he wasn't even sure he could define what a real life was anymore. So, why drag someone else into his confusion?

Easy answer. He didn't. Not even casually. Anything other than a passing glance and a wishful sigh got complicated, so he kept it uncomplicated, simple as that. The fewer lives he screwed up, the better.

On the other hand, being here was bordering on complicated since this was everything he was trying to put behind him. Medicine, unidentified outbreaks, epidemics…he wanted all of it out of his life. Problem was, controlling hospital-acquired infections, now called HAIs, was a growing specialty and the bigger problem in that was he was pretty good at what he did. It was hard to walk away from it when you were in demand. Harder still when he actually let himself think about the lives depending on his discoveries. But walking was what he'd been trying to do for the past two years. Walking, but always getting pulled back in.

So now, this Hospital de Caridad he was trying to find… He was promising himself it would be the last one. The last of the line for him, come hell or high water. Amanda Robinson had worked miracles with his nephew and this was paying back a debt of gratitude. Meaning, he'd find the HAI infecting the hospital she owned with her brother, then finally be done with it. Done with everything, without a clue what came after that.

Another mosquito dive-bombed Jack's ear, and he slapped at it, hitting it in midair. "You dirty little…"

"Dr. Jack Kenner?" a young voice piped up from the bushes just beyond the edge of the trail. "Are you Dr. Jack Kenner?"

"I'm Kenner," he said, quite surprised by an obviously adolescent voice. "Who are you, and does anybody know you're out here in the jungle alone?"

A scrawny scrap of a kid popped out of the bushes and walked right up to him. No shoes, no shirt, scraggly black hair, well-worn jeans, the biggest, widest smile Jack had ever seen on a face. "I'm Ezequiel," he said, extending his small hand to Jack. "I speak good English and I know all the roads and paths to the hospital. That's why they sent me to find you."

"That would imply I'm lost," Jack said, taking

firm hold of Ezequiel's hand, amazed and a little amused by the adult and purely unexpected gesture. "Which I'm not."

Ezequiel's grin didn't fade in the face of Jack's solid grip, or his denial. If anything, it widened. "Okay, then I'll go back and tell them you're on the wrong trail, but you're not lost." He pulled his hand back when Jack let go and crammed it into his pocket.

"How old are you, kid?"

"Twelve," he said. Then quickly added, "Almost."

Jack chuckled. Smart kid. Smart in his head, smart in the world. "And why do you speak English so well?"

"Missionaries used to teach me in school. I was the best student. Now the doctors and nurses teach me."

"Not surprised you're the best." Jack pulled a stainless-steel bottle of water from his backpack and offered it first to Ezequiel, who refused. Then he twisted off the cap, took a swig, and replaced the cap. "So, if I were to admit that I might be lost, how far, would you say, I'm off the trail I need to be on?"

"Far off," Ezequiel responded.

"If I'm that far off, how did you find me? Or even know where to look for me?"

"Everybody makes that mistake first time."

Yes, very smart in the world. He liked Ezequiel instantly. Saw that same gleam of youthful enthusiasm he used to see in Robbie's eyes. "Then I suppose I'm lucky you knew I might get lost."

"I didn't, but Doc Ben did."

Ben Robinson, Amanda's brother. Admittedly, he knew nothing about the man. Amanda hadn't said and he hadn't asked. Kept things the way he liked them—uninvolved. "And Doc Ben would be the one who sent the Jeep for me… The Jeep with a driver who dropped me off halfway here and pointed me in the direction of *Aldea de Cascada* rather than taking me all the way there?"

"We had an emergency, Doc K. Only got one Jeep."

Doc K? A nickname smacked of familiarity, and he didn't want familiarity of any kind coming anywhere near him. Especially not with another kid. Jack's nephew, Michael, was the only one he was going to allow in his life from now on. He was Cade's son, and there was safety in that relationship. He could get as close as he wanted yet keep the distance he needed. "Call me Jack, or Dr. Kenner,"

"Okay, Doc K," Ezequiel said, giving him the thumbs-up sign.

Choosing not to correct the boy, Jack shook his head in resignation. What the hell? He was only going to be here a day or two, then he was going back to Texas, back to wondering what came next. "So, how about you lead, and I'll follow?" Follow an almost twelve-year-old boy to a village hospital with one Jeep, an unidentified infection spreading, and God only knew what else. Sounded like a mess to him, but that pretty much summed up his life these days, didn't it? A real mess.

"Okay, so maybe I shouldn't have interfered, but you're in over your head here, Ben. And not asking anybody for help. Not even me, which has got me a little angry, to be honest." Amanda Robinson dropped her canvas duffel bag next to the bed, then plopped down on the lumpy mattress. Her home away from home. She loved it here, loved Caridad, didn't mind the lack of amenities. In fact, back in Texas, she found herself always counting off the days until she could return. "So I asked him, even though you didn't want me to. He was hanging around, working a few hours here and there at the hospital, and I took the opportunity when I saw it because Jack's the best in the field, and we have a problem he can fix. What did you expect me to do?"

"Let me handle it since I'm the one who actually runs the hospital."

"But I had Jack Kenner at my fingertips. I'd be crazy to ignore that." The way she hadn't been able to ignore him all these months. A man who made her toes tingle. Except, when she looked, he didn't look back. Hence a whole lot of unrequited tingling going on.

"And I have a computer with a connection to a satellite. These are modern times, Amanda. We have communication, even in the jungle, and I've been in touch with a couple people who are experienced in these kinds of infections."

"Okay, so maybe I overstepped…a little. But your people *aren't* Jack Kenner."

"You overstepped a lot." He sighed, then sat down on the edge of the bed next to his sister and wrapped a supportive arm around her shoulder. "But I'm glad you're here, interfering."

"Because I care," she said, her voice giving way to tenderness. "Your vision, my passion. That's why I work my butt off to support this place. You…*we* do important work." There might have been only a year separating them in age, and no real blood relationship between them, but Benjamin Thomas Robinson was the person she most admired in this world. What he'd overcome to get here… "And I'm sorry if this is going to cause a problem between us, Ben, but…"

"But you were taking care of me, the way you always have."

"I can't help it. That's just what happens, and you should be used to it by now."

He chuckled. "I am. And most of me appreciates your…hovering, nurturing, mothering, whatever you want to call it."

"Then we're good with this?"

"We're always good," he said, wrapping his other arm around her to give her a hug. "And I'm glad you're back. Ever since Dad died…"

"I know," she whispered, feeling her eyes dampen. "It throws everything off balance, doesn't it?" Ben was a Robinson by birth, she was a Robinson by adoption. But there'd been no distinctions in the family. They were tight-knit, loving. And her dad's death a few months earlier had changed things…. Things Ben didn't know. Didn't need to know. He had enough struggles of his own, without taking on hers. Which he would do, if he knew.

"Look, it was a long trip down here. Any chance that fantastic hospital cook might have a bowl of *guisos* left over from lunch?" At the mere mention of *guisos* Amanda found herself suddenly craving the thick meat and vegetable stew. It was a simple concoction, quite traditional here, and something she could easily make for herself back home—onions, garlic, veal, tomatoes, carrots, sweet potatoes, squash, rice... But in Argentina it tasted better. Satisfied a certain craving that wasn't about food—something she couldn't explain.

"Maybe afterward a *palmerita* covered in *crema pastelera?*"

A flat, circular pastry covered in a vanilla cream. "Are you trying to get on my good side?" she asked, sniffling back her tears. He was about courage, and it was always good to be with him, to work with him. Be inspired by his strength. "Because if you are, it worked."

"Well, I sent Ezequiel out to find your Jack Kenner. I got word he was coming in by commuter plane, so I asked Hector to go to the landing strip to get him but, apparently, there was an emergency over in Ladera. Someone needs transport to the hospital, and Hector let your friend out somewhere down the road, pointed him in the right direction, or shall I say *some* direction, since it's been a couple of hours. So I decided someone should go out and help him find his way."

A smile crept to Amanda's lips. Jack Kenner, lost in the jungle. Good-looking man. Rugged. Large. Black wavy hair, dark brown eyes, stubble on his chin, perpetual frown on his face... The thought of Jack lost out there, somewhere, was funny. To a point. Because that moment of amusement would be followed by the reality that Jack wasn't any too friendly most of the time, at least, most of *her* time, and she didn't see him being as amused by his predicament as she was. At best, he was aloof and she didn't know why, didn't really care to find out. She needed his skill, not his personality. Although something about that gruff personality invariably brought a sigh to her lips.

Still, Jack Kenner, lost... "He's not very personable, Ben," she said, straightening up, as her smile got larger.

"Yet look at you smile. Am I missing something here? Something about you and this man you haven't told me yet?"

"Nothing to tell," she said defensively, as the heat rose in her face. "I barely know him."

"So the blush doesn't mean anything?" he teased.

"I don't blush, and if I did, you wouldn't be able to see it."

"Scarlet red against your complexion…" He leaned back to appraise her, then grinned. "Haven't seen anything like that on you before, so he must be one hell of a man to do that to you, Amanda."

"I don't know anything about how he is as a man, just as a doctor."

"All I'm saying is—"

"Nothing, Ben. All you're saying is nothing, because there *is* nothing. And don't go trying to marry me off to this man when he gets here. Okay? Because last time you tried that…"

"I was thirteen, you were twelve."

"And he stalked me for half a year. Kept telling me you promised he could have me. Then I found out you *traded* me for that bicycle you said you found."

"Seemed like a fair trade at the time. And he did *love* you."

"Until he got a better deal."

"Yeah, well, love is fickle, isn't it?"

"Except I'm not in love with Jack Kenner. Not even in *like* with him. He's simply a means to an end for us, and I just wanted you to know, in advance, that he can be a little...abrupt."

"I've done some research. Saw a mention or two about his personality in some articles I read. And you're right. He's a pretty somber guy, apparently, but good. So, the rest of it doesn't matter, does it?" He arched teasing eyebrows. "Even a less perceptive man than I could read something into your blush, though."

She chose not to dignify her brother's implications anymore. He'd think what he wanted for now, and observe, in due course, how wrong he was. "No, Jack Kenner's attitude doesn't matter, except for poor Ezequiel. Jack's going to chew him up and spit him out."

"See, there you are. Another denial. Denial by ignoring what I just implied."

"Would you stop it? There's nothing going on. I asked him here because he's the best, and I was only trying to explain to you that his personality isn't always pleasant."

"Yet, you're attracted to that rough type, aren't you?" He chuckled. "Anyway, I think Ezequiel will hold his own against your friend." Ben smiled. Nodded appreciatively. "He's a resourceful kid."

"And Jack does love kids…" she said, hoping her brother would back off the teasing. The truth was, she was attracted. What woman wouldn't be? But how did you tell your brother it was purely physical? The answer: you didn't. "Even though he'll never admit to having a soft spot for anyone." Jack didn't wear his heart on his sleeve as a rule, but in a few of their encounters she'd seen it there. Which was why she'd turned to him when she'd realized her brother needed help. Jack cared. He did a pretty good job of hiding it—most of the time. But sometimes it slipped out. With his nephew, the emotion was obvious. "So, about that food I was begging for…"

Smiling, "Ah, yes. My sister's priorities."

"Your sister's priorities," she said, trailing him

out the door of the tiny hut she'd be calling home for the next couple of weeks. The only thing was, it wasn't really food she had on her mind. It was Jack Kenner. Back in Big Badger, Texas, he was a blunt force. But something about him being here in Argentina, in the jungle… That thought fascinated her almost as much as the jungle did. Almost.

Well, it was better than he'd expected. Nice little wooden structure. Probably ten or twelve beds in a central ward and a few private rooms. A small yet tidy surgery. Ample supplies. Well-kept grounds. Flowers planted here and there to give it a bright appearance. All of it perched on a little knoll overlooking the village called Aldea de Cascada.

Surprisingly, there were people milling around. Some appeared native to the area, some didn't. A few seemed to work here, others may have been visitors. All in all, he was more impressed by Hospital de Caridad than he'd expected to be. "Thanks for the tour, Ezequiel," he said, even more impressed by how the kid knew his way around the hospital. So, was it customary to tip the tour guide? He wondered about that since Ezequiel wasn't making a move to get away from him. In fact, if he hadn't known better, he might have thought the boy was latching on to him. "Is there something else we need to do?" he finally asked him.

Ezequiel shook his head. "Unless you want to see where you'll be staying."

"Sure. Show me."

"It's over there," Ezequiel said, pointing to a small hut adjacent to the hospital building.

It was nice enough. He'd stayed in far worse places, carrying out far worse duty, than what he was going to do here. "Okay," he said, still not sure what to do about Ezequiel. Then inspiration struck, and he slung his backpack off his shoulder and pulled out the stainless-steel water bottle. "You don't have one of these, do you?" he asked, holding it up.

Ezequiel shook his head.

"Then take it." He tried handing it over to Ezequiel, but the boy only looked perplexed.

"Back where I come from, when somebody gets lost, the person who finds them gets a reward."

"Reward?" Ezequiel questioned. "What's a reward?"

Jack thought for a moment, trying to come up with the right word to translate it. *"Recompense,"* he finally said. *"Regalo."*

"For me?" Ezequiel cried, sounding as excited as any child would who'd just received a gift.

Jack regretted he didn't have something better, something more suited for an almost twelve-year-old boy, and he wondered if he'd have an opportunity while he was here to find something else for Ezequiel. "Next time you have to go looking for someone…even if it's me…you can fill it with water and take it along in case you get thirsty." His second attempt to thrust the bottle at Ezequiel was met with success, and as soon as they boy latched on to it he opened it up and took a drink of the water still inside.

"Thank you, Doc K. I like it." Then the grin started, ear to ear. And Jack's heart melted. Damn it, he wasn't going to do that again. Wasn't going to get involved. Wasn't going to let another kid get to him. Not after Robbie, or Rosa. *Shift, refocus, get his mind off children.* Clearing his throat, Jack inhaled a deep breath. "Care to help me get settled in?"

Ezequiel frowned, again unsure of what Jack had just said. So Jack tossed him the backpack and motioned for him to come along to the guest hut. Okay, so maybe he wasn't here to make friends, but Ezequiel was turning into the exception, with that smile of his, and that unassuming nature. Besides, what did a couple of days' interaction with the kid hurt? Interaction didn't have to equate to involvement, did it? Especially if he kept reminding himself that in another few days all this would be behind him. "Then you can help me find Dr. Robinson, if you have time."

"He's in clinic now." He pointed to another hut, a much larger version of the hut he was headed to. "Over there."

Hospital de Caridad, translated to mean Charity Hospital, was like a small village in itself. A well thought-out place, keeping the clinic out of the hospital. Even though he hadn't yet met Amanda's brother, Jack was already beginning to like the man. Or at least appreciate his vision. The care and concern surrounding this hospital had been obvious to Jack almost the instant he'd stepped into the compound, and he hadn't even seen the actual hospital operation yet.

"Then that'll be our next stop, after we go in here." He stepped up to the door of the guest hut, which was an opening covered by mosquito netting, then pushed back the gauzy material and motioned for Ezequiel to go in first. Then he followed, got halfway into the hut, and stopped. "What the…?" he said, obviously surprised by who he found there. "You never said you were coming to Argentina, too."

Amanda, who was stashing a few clothes in the small bureau next to her bed, spun around. "Maybe not, but here I am anyway."

"Precipitated by what? Your need to keep an eye on me?"

"Don't sound so defensive, Jack. I'm inspired by your work. Wanted to watch it in progress."

"So you just packed up and came here on a whim."

"Yes, I just packed up. But you don't get to call it a whim."

"Why not?"

"Because coming to Argentina on a *whim* makes me sound irresponsible."

"There's something wrong with being irresponsible? Lots of people do it every day, and do it well."

"You sound like you believe irresponsibility could be an admirable goal."

"Not admirable. But definitely a goal for some people. Me included, if I get my way. And don't pull out your analyst's couch and tell me to lie down because there's nothing there you'd be interested in."

"Don't underestimate yourself, Doctor. I think I'd find plenty to interest me if you were stretched out on my couch."

"Let me guess. You're psychoanalyzing me, aren't you? Because my goal is not to have a goal." It was said with a certain amount of amusement, because the idea of boots off and under her analyst's couch was suddenly the only thing on his mind. Boots off, belt off, stethoscope off...

"I don't psychoanalyze. I treat conditions."

"And I'm a condition to treat."

"You're entitled to your opinion," she countered, her smile never breaking.

"My opinion is I'm the challenge you may want to take on, which is why you're here. But I'm also the challenge you won't crack, which is why I came."

"Faulty logic," she quipped. "You're here because you did crack under the challenge. Caved right in when I asked."

"Or agreed because there was a need for my services, as simple as that." Caved right in was more like it, but he wasn't about to give her the advantage of letting her discover she was right about him. Amanda was resourceful. She'd find a way to use that kind of information again. Which, on second thought, might be interesting. Too bad he didn't even go as far as interesting. "Oh, and in case you're interested, I'm impressed by your hospital."

"Changing the subject, Jack?"

He laughed. "You bet I am. It's safer that way."

Her smile didn't waver, but the edges around it softened. "Then the conversation is changed. Wouldn't want you feeling uncomfortable."

"Sounds like you're not really changing the conversation, just twisting it around to suit your purposes. Only my opinion, of course."

"My only purposes are what concerns the hospital. But Caridad is nice, isn't it?" she asked, taunting him with her eyes. "I'm proud of what Ben's done here. Which is why, when I'm running off to Argentina a few times a year, it may seem like a whim to some, but I'm actually here doing something I believe in with all my heart."

Something about her looked different. He studied her for a second, realized her hair wasn't twisted into its usual tight, librarianesque knot at the nape of her neck. It was loose, full of curl, wild. And her eyes had… The only way he could describe what he saw was *los ojos del fuego*. Eyes of fire. She was Amanda Robinson, but a different version from that he knew back in Texas. "So, I'm assuming we're roommates?" he said, turning around and walking over to join Ezequiel at his bedside.

"Yep, roommates. You over there, me over here, curtain down the middle." She bumped her bureau drawer shut with her hip, then grabbed a handful of clothes she'd left on the bed, and headed for a nook he figured had to be the bathroom. "You don't mind sharing, do you?" she called back over her shoulder, as she pushed back the door to the nook and walked into the room behind it. "Because the supply closet in the hospital isn't taken, if you'd rather have that. But you'd have to sleep sitting up."

"I'm fine," he said, kicking off his leather cowboy boots and letting them fly to the floor in the middle of the room.

"Good. Because the supply closet is a tight fit, especially if you're claustrophobic."

Except he wasn't claustrophobic. Right now, though, he was feeling a little gynophobic. Afraid of women. One woman in particular. Amanda Robinson was different, and that bothered him. What bothered him even more was that he was bothered about it in the first place.

In the tiny bathroom, the only place where'd she'd be able to find privacy in their living arrangement, Amanda leaned back against the door and drew in a deep breath to steady her nerves. She was shaking. Actually shaking…hands, knees, a few parts in between. So, what was that about? She knew Jack, had been the one to ask him here. Now, seeing him out of his Texas element… Even her breath was shaking as she shut her eyes and conjured up his image. Usual rough cut even rougher. Hair mussed, that sexy, *sexy* dark stubble on his face. Even the glisten of sweat on his face made him sexy. *Sexy…*

No! He couldn't be sexy. This wasn't about sexy.

Amanda's eyes flew open to stop the flow of pure sexual fascination with a man she was trying hard to repudiate as sexy. And failing miserably. Yet what had all that dialogue been about, especially the part where she had been getting him stretched out on her couch? Really? Was that what she'd said to him? Her analyst's couch, for heaven's sake!

Another round of shakes hit her because she didn't know what had come over her, and she didn't like it the least little bit that, rather than annoying her, his streak of opposition had tweaked something. Woken it up. Lit some kind of a fire.

It was like she was seeing Jack for the first time. Enjoying what she was seeing way more than she should. And now she was getting stressed out about sharing quarters with him, sleeping mere feet away from him. Forming an intimacy by proximity, something that had never bothered her all those years she'd slept in the hospital on call with colleagues and strangers alike. It was a bed, and everybody concerned was too tired to care who was in the bed across from theirs.

Except now she wasn't tired, and she did care, because... Well, it was the jungle. It was *always* the jungle, and the jungle always made her feel like someone other than who she was. Why? No clue.

But from the moment she arrived here—every single time she arrived here—the old Amanda started giving way to the new one. Sometimes it crept out of her by slow measures, sometimes it leaped, like a hungry panther.

Sure, there had to be a psychology to it, and as a psychologist she should have been able to figure it out. But maybe she liked the way she felt when she unpinned her hair and took off her pearls, which was why she avoided that little analysis. It just plain felt good to be Argentina Amanda.

So here she was, throwing off those figurative pearls by changing into something more comfortable than linen slacks and fitted blouse, anxious to get on with the panther inside her. Yet when she opened the door, she couldn't take that leap. That was the other Amanda fighting to take her back. The one who took control so completely now all she could do was stand in the doorway and stare at Jack, who'd apparently shooed Ezequiel away then stretched out flat on his bed. Either asleep already, or trying to bring on a self-induced trance.

She took a deep breath to calm herself, and to

help her hang on to the last few shreds of that other Amanda…shreds she was a little afraid to let go of. "Look, Ben's in clinic for another hour, and I'm on my way to the kitchen to see what I can find to eat. Care to come with me?"

"Thanks…not hungry," Jack said.

"Thirsty? There's always a pitcher of fresh lemonade."

"Not thirsty."

This was the way it was going to be? "Are you always so non-responsive?" she asked.

"Pretty much."

"Why?"

"Why not?"

"Because you're a doctor, and doctors are supposed to be responsive." He rose up, arched the sexiest eyebrows she'd ever seen in her life, and simply stared so hard at her she began to feel self-conscious. "What?" she finally asked.

He didn't answer, though. Instead, he lay back down and shut his eyes. Then finally said, "You're being responsive enough for the both of us. No need for me to join in and interrupt what you're doing so well."

Now he was playing with her. Look out, Jack Kenner. Because as sexy as he was to look at, he was just that challenging to be around, and she did love a good challenge. A thought that added just a bit more jungle wind to Amanda's sails as she tossed the clothes she'd been wearing down on her bed, then headed to the door of the hut. "Well, here's one more responsive moment from me, Jack. Those boots…keep them under your bed. Not in the middle of the floor. In fact, keep everything about you on your side. I don't like messiness."

"And I don't like fussy roommates. Which makes this a stand-off, doesn't it?"

"Not really," she said, smiling as she spun around and marched straight back to the middle of the room, where she bent down, picked up those boots then strode straight to the window, opened it and hurled them outside. "Not when there's a simple solution."

Jack's only response was to rise up again, give

her a good, hard stare, toe to head, then back down again. A stare so hard she could feel it graze her curves. Suddenly she was feeling self-conscious that her white shorts might be a little too short, or her white vest top a little too tight. Too much leg, too much chest.

"Okay, then," she finally said when Jack said nothing. "If you change your mind about that lemonade…"

By the time she was finally pouring that lemonade, she was back on course. Not as much as she wanted to be, though. Because that little episode in the guest hut, that up-and-down emotional swing—attracted, frustrated, attracted, frustrated—definitely wasn't her. These clothes weren't her. Nothing here was her. Not really. Yet it all felt so right. All except Jack, and she had no idea how what was going on inside her raised so many quivers, hackles, goose bumps and objections all at the same time.

The thing was, she knew she should avoid Jack. Maybe even wanted to. But could she? Truly, honestly, could she? And if she could, would she?

CHAPTER TWO

"I KNOW you're familiar with the basic concept, but let me give you a little background on hospital-acquired infections," Jack said, settling into a wooden chair across the table from Amanda, trying hard to regard her professionally. Not easy considering the way she looked.

"Believe me, I've been reading. And I think my brother has probably spent some time on his hands and knees trying to sanitize the ward. The thought of being sick because of something we're doing…" She shook her head. "We've got to stop it, Jack. Whatever it takes, we've got to stop it."

"Might not be what you're doing so much as what's being done to you," Jack said. "Everybody blames themselves, especially in smaller, more contained hospitals like Caridad, but these *bugs,* as I'll call them for lack of a better definition, aren't predictable, and just when you think you're on to something…" He shrugged. "Everything changes. Like life, in a lot of ways."

He studied Amanda for a moment, saw absolutely no resemblance to Ben whatsoever. While Ben was fair, she was so… His guess would have been Argentinian, actually. Possibly from the Pampas region, Mapuche descent, which she wasn't, of course. But maybe that was just what he wanted to see in her because her eyes were the same color as Rosa's, and her skin the same tone. Odd, how coming back after all this time affected him, seeing Rosa everywhere he looked.

"Anyway," he continued, shaking himself back into the moment, "internationally, the incidence of a hospital-acquired infection makes up nearly nine percent of all hospitalizations, with pediatrics being even higher than that. Unfortunately, in Latin and South America, more of these infections turn into critical situations than in most other areas in the world. And we're talking things like methicillin-resistant *Staphylococcus aureus,* an Enterobacter species resistant to ceftriaxone, and even Pseudomonas aeruginosa resistant to fluoroquinolones. To name a few."

Amanda pushed a can of soda in Jack's direction, and leaned back in her chair. "So what do we do about Caridad to keep this thing from spreading? It won't take much to shut our doors, and the area can't afford to have us shut down for even a little while because the next nearest medical service is about half a day away." She paused, took a drink of her own soda, then set the can down on the table. "This is killing my brother. He blames himself."

"But it's not his fault."

"Logically, he knows that. He feels responsible, though. That's the way he is, taking on everybody's problems. I mean, the first time I ever met him, there he was all stalwart in his new brother duties, showing me around the house, the yard, the neighborhood. You'd have thought he was going to be my adoptive father and not my brother. Yet he has that sense of purpose...."

She was adopted? So, maybe he was right. "It's human nature to feel responsible when we're sidelined the way Ben is right now. He sees his world falling apart and there's not a damned thing he can do about it. But he's lucky to have a sister who cares."

"You have Cade."

"Cade and I are only now becoming acquainted. I think that kind of relationship is a long way off for us."

"I hope it happens, because you're right. I'm lucky. Ben and I are as opposite as two people could be in most regards, which is pretty obvious, but we formed a tight bond almost instantly." She laughed. "After he quit trying to find ways to get rid of me. He sold me a couple times, traded me, and then there was the time he simply took me down the street to the neighbor's house and told me to wait on the doorstep until they came home, then tell them it was their turn to be my parents."

"Did you?"

She nodded, and her eyes softened. "And Ben got in so much trouble. But he felt threatened, having this new sister just drop in from nowhere. Maybe if my parents had adopted me when I was a baby..." Pausing, the slight smile of reminiscence dropped from her face. "Jack, you're pretty straightforward. I don't think you'd soft-pedal something to spare someone's feelings."

"That's a pretty low opinion of me."

"But I heard you at the hospital back in Texas, the way you talked to people, your interactions."

"I've been accused of being blunt."

"Then be blunt with me. Tell me what you see when you look at me. You've traveled extensively, lived in so many places around the world—South America, Africa, the Mediterranean regions. More than anybody I've ever known. So, when you look at me, do you see anything you recognize? A nationality? The hint of something you've seen before somewhere? Because of your background, I've wanted to ask you almost from the first time we met. But how do you simply blurt out something like that? And I'll admit I'm a little afraid to know."

"It wasn't in your adoption records?"

She shook her head. "There weren't any adoption papers, no records. Nothing."

Jack swallowed hard. But didn't answer.

"I've tried to find out. But the best I've come up with is that the adoption agency told my parents they believe I'm from some sort of Mediterranean background. Except…"

"Except you don't believe that."

"Except when I look in the mirror and want to believe that I am, the image looking back at me doesn't have a clue. But you do, don't you? You're trained to observe, and you don't miss things. That's what makes you the best in the world at what you do."

"Hospital infections and what you're asking me to do are two entirely separate things, Amanda," he said, not sure what to do with this. "What I do with a hospital infection is make a logical guess based on what I see, then do the tests to prove I'm either right or wrong."

"How often are you wrong?"

He shook his head. "Never," he said, clenching his jaw so hard the ache was starting to set in.

"Then make a logical guess based on what you see."

"Why me?"

She smiled. "Remember the first time we met? You asked for a list of my credentials, even though I'd already worked with your nephew for several months, and his parents were pleased with his progress. But there you were all big and blustery and none too friendly, making your demands. Then what I found out later… You actually called and checked me out. Asked every last reference on my list about me. Which was fine. I wish more people would do that when it comes to hiring the people who take care of their children. And while that really wasn't your responsibility since you're Michael's uncle, not his father, I liked that you were so forthright. Pegged you for a man who would always be honest, maybe sometimes brutally so. And you have your suspicions about my heritage, don't you?"

"I'm not even sure why you'd come to that conclusion."

"Because of the way you look at me. Sometimes you stare, and it's so…penetrating."

"The way a guy stares at a gorgeous woman, you mean?"

She shook her head. "That's not it. Oh, I've seen *that* look, more here than back in Texas. But that's not what I'm talking about. You give it away in your eyes, Jack. Not for long, but there's this flash… I saw it when I asked you. Saw it before that, actually."

She was probably right. What had caught him off guard, and what he'd tried to cloak, was that he saw Rosa in Amanda. Same eyes, same beautiful wild hair, same delicate bone structure. It was a look he wouldn't confuse with any other look in the world because the person he'd loved most had had that look. He'd come unglued, tried not looking, but sometimes couldn't stop himself. He was like a moth attracted to the flame. So if Amanda had caught that flash in his eyes, she'd caught it correctly. "Maybe this is something you should discuss with your family."

"I have. Too many times. Which is why I'm talking to you now. Why I'm asking you. Please, be honest with me, Jack. Respect me enough to do this one thing. When you look at me, who are you seeing?"

"A beautiful Mapuche woman." They were words he shouldn't have said, but words he felt bound to say because anything else bought into the lies that had cost Rosa her life. And for Rosa, he had no choice but to be honest.

"Mapuche?"

Nodding, he said, "Someone I loved once, a long time ago, was Mapuche. They're an indigenous people from the Pampas. I lived with them for a couple of years, working as a doctor in some of the villages."

"And you recognized that in me?"

"I did."

"Then thank you for your honesty."

"Amanda, I…"

She shook her head. "Just leave it where it is, Jack. I asked, you answered. It's what I wanted." More than that, it's what she needed, and she was numb with it, didn't know what to think, what to do. But Jack had given her something no one else ever had and for that she was grateful. "I think I always knew," she whispered.

"Knew what?" he asked gently.

"That what my parents told me was…off, some-how. Doesn't matter, though, does it?"

"Who we are always matters, Amanda."

"Or who we *aren't?* Anyway, I have a very im-portant date in a few minutes, so back to the prob-lem at Caridad. What's your plan?" She needed time to think about this, to readjust. To let the emotion catch up. But not here, not now. "And tell me what we can do to assist you."

"Are you sure? Because—"

She cut him off by nodding her head. "I'm sure." Not said convincingly enough, but Jack under-stood. The tone of his voice, the sense of concern emanating from him—yes, he understood.

"Fine." He paused, nodded. "But anytime you want to talk…"

"The hospital, Jack. Please, make this about the hospital now." No matter how distanced she was feeling from everything she knew.

"Well, then, no more cleaning, to start with. I need to find the source of contamination before I do anything else, then culture it to see what grows. Which means I'll look in all the usual places and get creative after that because in my experience the usual places don't really yield what I want."

"It's an odd specialty."

"But, as they say, someone has to do it."

"Why?"

"Public health was always what I wanted to do. You know, take care of the people no one else wanted to take care of."

"Because of Robbie?" she asked. Jack's brother Cade had told her once about Robbie, about how his parents hadn't wanted to raise a child with severe autism.

"You know about my brother?"

She nodded. "The child nobody wanted."

"After he died, I wanted to find a way to take care of people who were overlooked the way he was. He died because no one noticed him."

"He ran off, didn't he?"

Jack nodded. "No one saw that he had been missing for a while and he wasn't found until it was too late. When I became a doctor I wanted to make a difference for people who, like Robbie, weren't noticed until it was too late, which was why I chose public health. What I do now grew out of that as conditions in some of the places I chose to work in weren't good. So, you'd cure the patient and find the source of the illness in so many cases—fleas, ticks, four-legged critters, bacteria."

"But you quit or, at least, you've stepped away for a while, haven't you? That's what Cade told me. He said it's why you were hanging around Big Badger, why you were thinking about working with them at the hospital they were starting."

"You're right. I've stepped away. Not sure if I'll go back and work at the hospital, or not. Haven't decided…personal reasons. It's complicated."

Personal reasons he wouldn't divulge. She could see it in his eyes, like she could see the well-practiced resistance there, as well. Jack had given her what she'd wanted and now it was her turn to do the same. She'd broached a subject he didn't want to talk about, so she wouldn't pry. As a psychologist, it was her second nature to ask, especially when she saw so much distress. But for Jack she would go against that nature. It was the least she could do.

"Okay, well… You have free rein here, Jack. Whatever you need to do is fine, and if I can help you, let me know. We do have some funds…" She stood, then spun around to the beat-up old refrigerator behind her, opened it and grabbed a pitcher of juice—apple-pear mix from Patagonia. "But not a lot. So whatever you can do to be conservative would be appreciated. And right now I'm going to go have juice in the garden with Maritza Costa. Ventricular septal defect. Congenital." Meaning, a small hole in her heart. "She's feeling better today, and I think a nice walk in the fresh air will do her good."

"You're treating her how?"

At the mention of a child with a heart condition Jack's face turned to stone. Amanda saw it, saw the visible change come over him. Such a drastic turnabout, it made her curious. One curiosity among many, she was only beginning to discover. "With medicine only, for the time being," she explained. "And observing her. She got sick, probably a cold, and it lingered, so her parents brought her in and that's when Ben made the discovery. She's been a normal, healthy little girl, without any cardiac problems. So we're being cautiously optimistic we can keep her regulated with the most conservative treatments, because we can't convince her parents to let us send her to another facility for more sophisticated testing, maybe even surgery."

"What about a cardiac cath? They use them more and more these days to close small holes, and it's a safe procedure. Proving itself worthy of the task."

"Maybe it is," she continued, "if we had the means to perform a cardiac catheterization, which we don't. That equipment's on the list of things we hope to be purchasing in the next year or so."

"So in the meantime…"

"We keep a close eye on her and try to keep her as healthy as we can."

"Or go argue some sense into her parents."

"Believe me, Ben would have done that months ago if he'd thought it would work. But we have to

maintain the balance here, because the people...
While they want the medical help, they're always
a little suspicious of outsiders."

"A little?" he snapped. "They'd let that child die
because they're a little suspicious?"

"She's not critical, Jack. And we're doing the
best we can."

"But what happens when your best isn't good
enough anymore?"

It was a rhetorical question. She knew that, and
decided to let it pass. "Look, it makes me angry,
too. And my brother paces the floor he worries
so much. But that's the way we have to do things
here, because we want to get along. It's for the
good of everyone, including Maritza. Things are
changing here in the way we're accepted, and
those changes have their own pace. I mean, you
lived here, so you already know that. Probably
better than I do."

"Look, I'm sorry. You have a nice facility here
at Caridad, I'm not criticizing it. And I'm not criticizing either you or Ben. What you have works,
and it's none of my business how you treat your

patients, so forget what I said because I'm not the one trying to take care of medical services on so many levels with so few means."

Amanda stepped closer to Jack. "I appreciate the concern. No apologies necessary for that. And, Jack…thank you for earlier, for telling me who I might be." She bent and kissed his cheek, her voice catching as the words came out. "Sincerely, thank you."

As she was leaving, Ben was entering, and she gave him a bye-bye wave as she flitted out the door like a butterfly on a light breeze.

"She's…" Jack shrugged, not able to come up with the right word to describe her.

"A force," Ben supplied.

"A force," he repeated, just a little bowled over by Amanda's passion. She was so out there about it. In his life those kinds of emotions were kept hidden, and he wasn't used to being around someone like her, who showed all of it so naturally. It was a little off-putting to that self-admitted stodginess in him he tried to sustain. But it was also fascinating, much more than he would have expected. Still, should he have told her who she might be? It bothered him, made him uneasy being put in that position. Part of him was already realizing, though, that turning her down in anything she asked was going to be tough. Maybe damn near impossible. Because she *was* a force.

"Anyway," he went on, trying to shake Amanda from his mind, "about this hospital-acquired infection you've got going…"

"Seven diagnosed cases right now, all of them limited to the children's ward. General symptoms but not that serious—abdominal pain, nausea, vomiting, malaise."

"Fever? Cough?"

"Not yet. And the good news is we can do a limited amount of cultures here. But the bad news is, since we're not really set up for it, I'm not sure I'd totally trust the results, if we were getting results, which we aren't."

"Which means everything's turning up negative?"

"No positive test results for anything we've cultured. We're set up to treat patients, and our lab, well… Let's just say you're not going to be impressed with it. So let's just get this tour over with so you can figure out what to do with what we've got."

"You mean Ezequiel's tour wasn't a real tour?" Jack asked, smiling. "Great kid, by the way. Smart."

"We're fond of him."

"It's good you let him hang around. Gives him a purpose."

"And a home," Ben commented.

"He lives here?"

"For a little over a year now. His mom brought him with her when she came for treatment, but she died from cancer, and we couldn't find anybody who knew Ezequiel, let alone wanted him. No relatives, no family friends. So we set up a room for him…turned a large storage closet into a room, actually, and we all keep an eye on him. Make sure he's fed, clothed."

"Then he's one of the lucky ones," Jack said, thinking about Amanda, who'd also been one of the lucky ones. Thinking about Rosa, who hadn't been.

"Lucky maybe, but he's not getting a proper education, which is a problem. We're each taking turns teaching him, but there's no consistency to it. And he's not with a family, not getting that kind of nurturing, which is an even bigger problem, because all kids need that. Yet if we turn him in to the authorities we might as well give him up for good. He's too old to be adopted, probably wouldn't do well in an institutional situation, which is where he'd end up if he didn't run off. So we just…"

"Look the other way and hope for the best."

Ben cringed. "When you put it that way, it sounds bad, doesn't it?"

"No. Not really. I've worked in a lot of difficult situations and seen these lost children everywhere. Ezequiel's sharp. A real survivor. You're giving him more than he would have any other way, and he'll make it through."

"Let's hope so, but he deserves better. Anyway, welcome to our lab," Ben said, pushing open a door to reveal a closet-size space, set up with a table and two antiquated microscopes. "Like I said, don't expect much. I found these in storage in a public hospital in Buenos Aries. They'd upgraded, and told me to help myself. So I filled our communal Jeep with everything I thought we might be able to use, which makes us, officially, a hand-me-down hospital." Said with a big smile.

"I think the term today is repurposed." Jack stepped in, took a quick look, and decided it would work. Not well, but well enough for some basic cultures. "So, Amanda said I have free rein, which means I'd like to start by examining the ward where the kids have been infected."

"Well, since pediatrics is Amanda's specialty, she's going to assist you once she's done with Maritza. Oh, and while you're here, I've taken the liberty of adding you to our clinic schedule, if that's okay with you."

"You're good, slipping that in there when you think I'm focusing on something else," Jack said, laughing.

"We take our advantages where we can." He

patted Jack on the back. "Anyway, I'm glad you're here, and until I hear otherwise, I'm going to consider you on call for general duty, starting tonight." Ben pointed to the door at the opposite end of the hall. "My sister's out there, when you're ready for her."

Jack didn't respond. Could anyone every really *be* ready for Amanda?

Slipping into a pair of plum-colored scrub pants, Amanda cinched the drawstring at the waist and headed for the pediatric ward. Actually, it wasn't a ward so much as one large room, sparse with equipment and other medical accoutrements. But there were beds, and sick children, and a growing problem that worried her.

Funny how Jack's mere presence brought with it peace of mind. She couldn't deny it, particularly since some of that peace was oozing into her. Peace in her medical life and, oddly, peace in her personal life. It was better knowing she might be Mapuche, she'd decided. Painful because that knowledge caused uncomfortable questions, but better. Although she owed him an apology because clearly he hadn't wanted to be involved in the disarray she called her personal life. Yet he'd allowed himself to be dragged in, which wasn't at all what she'd expected from him.

Something had changed him, though. She'd seen it happen. Seen the incredible struggle when it had flashed over him. But he had been so quick to grab it back, put it away. Leaving her wondering about the person he'd loved. Someone Mapuche. Perhaps a woman? The love of his life?

It occurred to her Jack may have returned to Argentina bearing some kind of pain, simply because she'd asked. "Who are you, Jack?" she asked, as her scrub top slid into place. "What kind of man are you?"

The kind who would fight to keep her from figuring him out. That was the answer that came to her on her way to meet him in Pediatrics. He wanted his distance, and she wanted… Well, she wasn't sure about that. Maybe all she wanted was to understand him. After all, their worlds did intersect in more than one place, so why wouldn't she want to understand someone who threaded in and out? Yes, that was it. A perfectly good reason for having Jack on her mind almost constantly. Which had turned into the case.

All thoughts led to Jack, but that was okay, because all she wanted was to understand. That was some mighty fine logical reasoning leading up to a half-believed conclusion. Who was she kidding, though? Because peel back all that logic and she just plain liked his gruff exterior, even his distance. That was what Argentina did for her, gave her different freedom than she was used to. Changed her perspective. It happened every time she was here, maybe because deep down she'd always felt the innateness of who she was. Or wanted to be.

"Anything going on other than what's being recorded in the charts?" Jack asked from his casual seat behind the old wooden desk that sufficed as the hub of the ward. One desk, one swivel chair, a rusty file cabinet, all of it tucked into the corner, out of the way. And Jack's size overwhelmed everything. An immense man in a small space made the man look even more immense.

Amanda noticed that, fought to keep her gaze steady. "Not really. Symptoms are mild, nothing you wouldn't expect. No one critical or even in danger."

"And you don't think that this might be some run-of-the-mill hospital infection, one that's not going to cause any real trouble." It was a statement, not a question. "Ben's downplaying it, so he's not the best one to go to for an objective answer. You, though, got me here, which means you're worried. So what's your assessment?"

"That's just it, Jack," she said, perching herself on the edge of the desk. "I don't know. Ben's been fighting this HAI for a few weeks now, it's isolated, but it's not going away. Not getting better or worse, either. With the way things mutate… and I'm not the expert on this, so bear with me. But you read how these various strains, bacterial and viral, mutate, and how so much of what we thought would stop the spread is rendered ineffective very quickly. My brother is smart, and he'll do whatever it takes to protect the hospital. Me too, because I'm also involved in this, and I believe you're what it takes or else I wouldn't have asked for your help."

"Well, for what it's worth, every hospital known to man runs some sort of HAI strain through it, Amanda. These kids have gastrointestinal flu-like symptoms. That's all. And according to what I've read, they've all been cured pretty easily."

"But per patient, our percentage is huge. One third of them are coming down with something we're giving them and that statistic, if nothing else, should be a warning. It's just that I don't know what the warning is about."

"Then it's a good thing you called me because warnings are my specialty." He glanced up. "So, it's time for me to meet the ward."

"Not the children?"

"Nope, not at first," he said, standing. "Sometimes not at all. I seem to have a better rapport with the contaminant than I do patients, so I try to keep to where I'm better received."

"Such a low opinion of yourself," she said.

"Or a high one, depending on your perspective. Anyway, with the symptoms that are manifesting themselves, the scope of what could be infecting the kids should be pretty limited, so I like to look at everything from a fresh perspective, which includes culturing areas that wouldn't normally be associated with what we're seeing. In other words, wear a sturdy pair of suspenders along with a belt, just in case."

"Overreacting?" she asked, smiling.

He didn't answer her at first. Instead, he merely stood and stared at her, eventually giving in to a half smile, then finally, "Reacting."

"Okay, then. If you're intent on reacting, did you bring the testing supplies with you, because we don't have—"

"I come prepared. Might even have another trick or two up my sleeve." He grabbed his white lab coat off the back of the chair, which she hated seeing because she liked his look now...cargo pants, and a crisp, white T-shirt. But everybody had something to cover up, didn't they? Jack covered something dark and despairing. Her parents covered something that scared her. She covered up so many things in herself, as well.

But what would happen once the covers started to peel back? That was a question she couldn't answer. And wasn't sure she wanted answered.

CHAPTER THREE

"I DON'T suppose you've solved it already?" Amanda asked hopefully. "You know, one swipe of a trusty test swab and you have your answer." She plopped down on her bed, flat on her back, and looked across at Jack, who was busy reading, also trying hard to ignore her. "You know, Jack, the kids I work with back in Texas don't respond to me half the time for any number of reasons. They're slow processing the question, not sure what an appropriate response is. A lot of the time they're distracted, or they simply don't know that answering when someone asks them a question is the right thing to do. So when I don't get a response from them, I understand because my children, for the most part, are autistic, and I teach them how to respond. But you don't need to be taught."

He turned his head to look at her, not even bothering to push up the reading glasses that had slid halfway down his nose. "Your point being?"

"We're roommates. Roommates talk to each other."

"I don't have roommates, and if I did, we wouldn't have anything in common to discuss."

"Oh, I think you would, and a great place to start would be why you always set yourself apart from everybody else. People think you've got a terrible personality, that you're unfriendly or grumpy. I heard that about you all the time back in Texas, from my own receptionist, from hospital staff. But do you know what I think?"

"Could I stop you from telling me if I *didn't* want to know?"

"Just ask. I'll respect your wishes." True to form, he did what she expected. Ignored her for about thirty seconds. Then he finally pushed his glasses back up, specifically so he could look over the tops of them at her.

"Then don't tell." He cracked a half smile. "Or do. Whichever makes you happy."

She laughed. "So that's how you want to be?" He was like a breath of fresh air. No rules, no concern for what others thought of him. Basically, a man on his own terms, and she liked that.

"No, that's how I am. I learned a long time ago it's easier to let people just do what they want to do. It makes them happy, which makes my life a whole lot less complicated when it involves me. Besides, human nature… When someone asks you if you want to know what they think, they're going to find a way to tell you."

"Better watch out, Jack. You could be giving me insight into who you are, which means that if I do tell you what I think, I might be saying something you don't want to hear."

"Yeah, right. Like I haven't heard it all before?"

"Not from my perspective, you haven't."

"Human nature again. While you think your perspective of me may be unique, it isn't."

"But you won't know that until I tell you what I think."

"Which leaves the ball in your court. Tell me, or don't tell me. Either way…" He held up his journal. "Reading. Seven articles to catch up on. All of them on the HAIs *du jour.* You know. What's trendy, what's new, what's coming back into style."

She studied him for a moment, and saw something that surprised her. Devilment, maybe? Was he actually playing with her? "You don't ever just make the best of it, do you?"

"The best of what?"

"Your situation. The people you're with. You know, occupy your moment. This is Argentina, Jack. Argentina! It's Friday night, barely dark. We're in the holiday season now, and the people in the village are starting their celebrations. Making the best of your situation would be going down to the village, joining in or at least observing from one of the outside tables at a cantina. Talking to people, letting people talk to you. You know, having fun."

"You think reading medical journals isn't fun?"

"I think you're hiding behind a bunch of journals because you know you *will* have fun if you step out."

"Then you're challenging me."

"Not so much challenging you as…"

"Purposely distracting me."

"No. I'm telling you what I think."

"See, I was right. You wanted me to know, so you sneaked it in there when you thought I wasn't paying attention."

"Oh, you were paying attention. I doubt there's ever a time in your life when you don't."

He was definitely one tough nut to crack. Still, she wasn't giving up on him, and it had nothing to do with professional camaraderie. She just plain wanted to see Jack unwind. Wanted to see what he'd be like when his mind wasn't on such weighty things.

Okay, she was attracted on some weird level. She'd admit it. Back in Texas, the first time she'd met him, that attraction had crept up on her, but there had been nothing she could do about it as he'd been a family member of one of her patients. Yet here, in Argentina, they were doctor to doctor, and that attraction level was turning into something more than she'd expected.

"Oh, and fun is what you want it to be, Jack. If spending a dull evening reading journals is your type of fun, my brother's got boxes of them when you get done with these. But if you want to go meet the people here, mingle a little, see what makes them who they are, then fun is where I'm going, and you're invited along—to participate, or simply observe." Okay, maybe she was trying to distract him a little. Nothing serious, and not for long, though.

"Except I'm on call."

"So am I, but we're not going that far. And we've got adequate staff on to take care of anything routine that arises." She rolled over on her right side to face him, and propped her head up with her hand. "At a leisurely stroll we can be back here in ten minutes. Running, in less than two. Any more excuses?"

"Give me a minute to think, okay?"

"Said as the man is sitting up and putting his glasses on the table next to the bed. Which means you're coming to the village with me. Right?"

"Or getting ready to explore your brother's boxes of journals."

"Ah, yes. The way Argentinian Friday nights are meant to be spent."

"Are you goading me, by any chance?"

"Not goading. Just…" She paused, thought for a moment, wrinkled her nose when she couldn't come up with an answer.

"See, I was right, wasn't I? You *are* trying to distract me."

"Or show you something beneficial."

"Beneficial? How so?"

"A night off clears your head, lets you relax…"

"Oh, so we're weighing more medical knowledge against a night of bright lights and music? Now I understand." He gazed across at her for a minute—a solid gaze that gave away no aspect of himself whatsoever—then shut his journal. "I had this relationship once, back in medical school. Fine-looking woman. One of my professors, actually. At the end of her day she was done. She could go home, kick off her shoes, read a book, cook a meal, do whatever she wanted to do."

"Which was you, I'm guessing."

He arched a suggestive eyebrow at her. "The only problem with that was at the end of my day I had to work a part-time job to keep myself in medical school. When I wasn't delivering pizzas, I was studying. When I wasn't studying, I was sleeping. So I got maybe two hours with her, which gave her cause to think that we could have our *benefits* any old time she wanted them."

"You're comparing me to her?"

"Nope. Just saying two hours, that's all."

"What?" she sputtered, laughing. "The moral to your story is that I get two hours? I was expecting…"

"Something deep and profound, with a meaning that summed up the moral good? Sorry, I was just telling you that if you want me to go to the village with you, we'd better do it now because I still have reading to do."

In reaction, Amanda rose up, picked up her pillow and hurled it across the room at him, hitting him square in the face. "Want to know what I think?" she asked, standing up.

Jack groaned as he pushed himself off the bed. "Could I stop you from telling me if I didn't want to know?"

She produced a second pillow from behind her back, lobbed it at him, hit him in the face again. Then laughed. "Fun, Jack. That's what I think. In spite of yourself, you're going to have fun."

It was a few weeks until Christmas, and the village was already ablaze with lights strung everywhere. Some of them blinked, some didn't. There were lights hanging on bushes and trees, on house eaves, on fences and trash cans. Parked cars were decked with lights, as was furniture that had been dragged to the yard for sitting on outside on a hot summer night. Even a little terrier trotting up the main street behind a group of revelers sported blinking lights on his collar. All in all, the main street of the village took on an orange-red glow. "If I stop, are they going to string me with lights?" Jack asked Amanda.

"It's beautiful, isn't it?" she said, her voice filling with emotion. "Such a simple thing, yet it unites the village. Gives people the chance to come together, and be part of something bigger than the village itself."

Beautiful wasn't about the lights. What was truly beautiful was her reaction to everything around her, and watching her play in the middle of it all. "It's beautiful," he replied. Amanda had this effervescence about her, and it was catching. Even as he resisted being caught, he could feel himself bring dragged in. Disconcertingly, not kicking and screaming as he was being dragged.

"Then you do like it!" she exclaimed. "Because I knew I could find a sentimental spot in you somewhere."

"Sentimental is stretching it. Let's just say that I can appreciate what I'm seeing for its very nice attributes."

"But wouldn't that suggest a certain sentimentality for the holiday?"

More like a certain appreciation for what the holiday seemed to bring out in her. Which, of course, he wouldn't bother mentioning. "When I was a kid growing up, our Christmases were boring. Very regimented. One tree, all lights and ornaments the same color, packages wrapped to match the tree had to be lined up underneath according to their size. We weren't allowed to pick them up or shake them to guess what was inside. Weren't even allowed to be in the same room with the tree without adult supervision for fear we'd disturb something on it."

"Then it's time to make a new holiday memory for you. Something to balance out the bad one."

"That's assuming I want to balance it out."

"Don't you? I mean, don't we all want to balance out the bad memories, maybe even replace them totally with something better?" She tugged him to a stop, then pointed to a man stringing lights on his blueberry bush. "So, let's make a memory, Jack. Right now it may not seem like much to you, or even worth the effort, but maybe someday, when you look back, you'll feel differently."

She was trying so hard on such a lost cause. And he *was* a lost cause. But not so lost that he had the heart to tell her she was wasting her time. Honestly, he liked being with Amanda probably more than he'd liked being with anyone in a good long time. It would be short-lived, once she got to know him better and found him not quite the cause she'd thought him to be. But for now, who knew? Maybe there *would* be a good memory involved. "Why the blueberry bush?" he asked.

"Here, they celebrate the blueberries with decorations. It's a few weeks past the harvest, but in Aldea de Cascada people leave the berries on their personal bushes as long as they can so they can be ready for *El festival de los arándanos.* Festival of the blueberries."

"Which is?"

"What we're celebrating right now. A fairly new festival, but…" She pulled away from Jack, ran into the yard and picked up a strand of lights to help the man, named Alberto, with his decorating. "An important one," she called back. "Blueberry farming is new to the area, and it's turning into an important business. Here, in Aldea de Cascada, they pay homage to their good fortune by celebrating the blueberries." She gestured to another strand of lights on the ground, then nodded at a second berry bush. "And they like to party for any occasion, so it works out."

"So, if I string these lights on the berry bush, what's in it for me?" he asked, trying to hold on to a frown that simply wouldn't be held on to.

"The satisfaction of knowing you contributed to the pleasure of others."

"But staying back and reading my journals contributes to the quality of life of others."

She laughed. "And now you're being obstinate for the sake of being obstinate, aren't you?"

Rather than answering, Jack grabbed up a strand of lights, stepped up to the bush, plugged the end of the strand of lights into the lights on the other bush, then watched the colors light up. Reds, yellows, greens, blues…and all for a berry bush. "Not obstinate. Just stating the obvious," he said, as he started twining the lights about the bush.

"But aren't you missing something with that attitude?" Amanda countered. "You allow yourself to touch humanity, yet you don't allow it to touch back. Just look at the beauty we can create around us as humans. Beauty you may have part of, but won't let be part of you."

"It's a string of lights on a blueberry bush. Pretty by some definitions, useless by others."

"It's a festival, Jack. Very pretty and probably as useless as it is pretty. But you know what? Every time you look at a blueberry, for the rest of your life, you're going to have a memory of the festival celebrating it. And it's going to be a pleasant memory because, in spite of yourself, you're having a good time. Or else, why would you be stringing lights on a blueberry bush?"

He chuckled. "There's fault in that logic somewhere. Just not sure where."

"But I'm right. Admit it."

"You're right in that I'll have a memory." But of something much better than a blueberry.

"Good. Then let's go see what other kinds of memories we can make." For their efforts, Alberto presented them with a small basket of blueberries, and Amanda immediately popped one into her mouth. "Sweet," she said, plucking one out and offering it to Jack, who shook his head in refusal.

But Amanda wouldn't take no for an answer. She held it out again, and he refused again.

"You're going to eat this berry, Jack," she said, waving it at him. "One way or another, you're going to eat it."

"Oh, the mere scrap of a woman is going to force it down my throat?" he asked, quite amused by her determination.

"The mere scrap of a woman will pin you to the ground if she has to," Amanda countered, taking a step closer.

Her eyes simply sizzled with the challenge—a sizzle that started to catch fire in him. "All by yourself?"

"I've tackled them bigger than you."

An image that turned the fire into pure, pounding arousal. "What if I told you I'm deathly allergic to blueberries?" he asked, struggling to conjure up a focus on anything but Amanda. Images of trees and water and birds popped into his mind then kept on going, as hard as he tried clinging to them. Then he centered upon surgical instruments, and surgical procedures and postsurgical therapies, but none of that worked either, because as something popped into his mind's eye, Amanda came after it, taking a sexy hip-swing to it and knocking it away.

"What if I told you you're lying, that I can see it in your eyes?" She took another step closer. Stopped. Held out the blueberry. Then took another step. "Come on, Jack. Give in. One blueberry, and I'll leave you alone."

Except he wasn't sure he wanted to be left alone. "See, that's the thing. When you challenge me like you're doing, I can't give in. It's not in my nature."

"Or in mine."

"So we're at an impasse?" he asked, as she took two more steps, then stood so close to him that one inch farther and she would have been pressed into his erection.

"Not an impasse," she said, as she quickly raised her hand to his face to claim her victory. But instead he claimed her hand. Caught her by the wrist and held her hand mere inches from his lips, her fingers still clinging to the berry. "Victory."

"Mine, or yours?" he asked, his voice too thick

to pretend anything other than the raw sexual energy between them.

"Depends," she purred.

And in that moment, he let his guard down just enough that she was able to slip the blueberry between his lips, and whether it was the blueberry that tasted so sweet to him or her finger lingering on the tip of his tongue just a moment longer than it should have as he devoured the berry, he wasn't sure. It didn't matter, though, because... victory. It was his. And, yes, it was sweet.

"See, Jack. That's what's in it for you. Something sweet."

Trying to regain his bearings, his senses and hopefully a little sensibility, he let go of Amanda's wrist and stepped backward. While his head wasn't spinning, everything else in his world was right then and it was time to stop it. Time to be Jack Kenner again and not the idiot who went all goofy over Amanda's persuasion.

"Sweet or not, your two hours are ticking away." She popped another blueberry in her mouth, didn't bother offering him one, then latched on to Jack's arm again. "Your two hours, Jack. These are *your* two hours. So let's go buy a strand of lights and find something of our own to decorate."

In his state of mind, with the throbbing in his groin not yet abating, all he wanted to do was go off somewhere and smoke a cigarette, and he didn't even smoke. "But I thought this was supposed to be my two hours. If that's the case, shouldn't I get to choose what we do?" A myriad of thoughts on that subject went through his mind, and not a one of them had anything to do with stringing lights.

"Under normal circumstances, yes. But this is my gift to you, which means I get to choose what it is."

She pointed to a vendor making his way up the road with a pushcart. Children were following the vendor, trying to get a peek at the goods he had for sale, while old ladies were scurrying to keep up with the procession, endeavoring to get a bargain. Not far ahead, a makeshift street band, made up of a saxophone, an accordion and a guitar player, rendered their version of popular Christmas carols while a grizzled old man peddled tamales and empanadas from the street corner.

"The vendor has lights. My treat. But since these two hours are yours to spend, you've got to decide what to decorate with them." She smiled as she chose three strands with mixed colors from the cart, and handed a five-peso bill to the merchant, waving him off when he tried to render change. "Does it seem like a good compromise?" she asked Jack, who was backing farther and farther away from the cart with each passing second.

"Do I have a choice?" he shouted, trying to sidestep a parade of revelers coming his way, all of them decked out with homemade kazoos and drums. Too late, though, for Jack, who got swept into the procession, was totally surrounded by at least a dozen music-makers who latched on to him like leeches, then pulled him into the bosom of the band as it marched its way on down the street.

Amanda stood there for a moment, watching Jack being literally swept away in a festive wave, a little surprised and very pleased he wasn't trying to forcibly remove himself from the merry-making cluster. But he wasn't. He was simply, and quite literally, going with the flow. He wasn't exactly interacting with the people around him, or giving in to the dancing or the tin noisemaker being offered him. But he was going with them, nonetheless.

"You really find him fascinating, don't you?" Ben asked, stepping up behind her.

"I'm not sure why. But, yes, I do."

He handed his sister a cup of yerba *mate* tea, a traditional herbal concoction known as a national favorite. "Well, maybe it's something about the lure of an unobtainable man. You know, wanting what you can't have."

"Spoken by the most unobtainable man I know," she said, lifting the drink to her lips. Stimulating, odd, definitely an acquired taste. One of the things she actually looked forward to when she visited.

"And you've put *yourself* out there to be obtained?"

She shifted her gaze to Ben, her lips still on the cup. "What's that supposed to mean?"

"I think you know exactly what it means. If you like the guy, go get the guy."

"How's that going to work when the guy doesn't want to be got? And that's assuming I even want to get him. Which I don't."

Ben actually laughed. "Good try, but I'm not buying it. I've seen the way you look at him."

"What if I do? I admire him, sure. I'm a medical doctor, he's a medical doctor, so I'm allowed to. What's wrong with that?"

"Again, I'm not buying it. You brought that look in your eyes with you to Argentina this time, which tells me this *thing* between you, or some variation on the theme, has been going on for a while."

"You're wrong, Ben. I mean it. You're totally wrong about what you're thinking."

"Maybe I am. Maybe I'm not."

She shrugged him off. "Then think whatever you want to, however wrong it is, while I go and rescue Jack. He's not enjoying the poncho and *boina* someone just put on him." *Boina,* meaning beret.

"And I think you're being too attentive for someone who's not interested in the guy with the poncho. So on that note I'm going back on duty."

"Yeah, run away instead of facing the fact that you're wrong."

"The lady doth protest too much, methinks."

"Methinks you should go away, Ben."

"I will, but it doesn't solve a thing."

"You two fighting?" Jack asked, handing her his *boina*. He'd already rid himself of the poncho somewhere in the crowd.

"Disagreeing. Not fighting," she said, putting the *boina* on her own head. "It's a long-standing tradition between us. He thinks he knows what's best for me and I tell him how wrong he is."

"Is he ever right?"

"Occasionally."

Jack smiled. "Then sometimes you *do* give in. That's good to know."

"Only about some things. But not the lights. Have you thought how you want use them?"

"You're still on that kick?"

"It was part of the plan, remember?"

"I don't make plans," he said. "They get too complicated, and usually take you in directions you don't want to go."

"But couldn't they take you in a direction you want to go or, better yet, need to go, even if you don't know it at the time?" She spied a couple of empty seats at a tiny tile-topped table in an adjacent cantina, grabbed hold of Jack's arm and dragged him across the street, then sat down. Except Jack didn't sit. He stopped just short of the little outdoor café and simply stood on the road and looked at her.

"Okay, you're right. So, I made a plan for my lights," he finally told her.

She knew exactly what it was going to be. Jack was going to pitch them into the nearest trash can, or shove them in the direction of the next person who strolled by him. Which totally mucked up her plans for the evening because no matter how much she wanted Jack to be part of this, it wasn't going to happen. He might go through the motions, but none of this was him, and that disappointed her. What had she expected, though? Take him to the festival and witness a miraculous transformation? Time to let Jack be Jack again. "Fine, take them," she said, trying to hide her disappointment.

"You coming with me?"

To face her failure in something where she was so positive she was right? Not a chance. "You go on. I've still got some party left in me." Party for one. And on a very blue note.

"I can come back later and walk you to the hospital," he offered.

She shook her head. "I'm fine."

He held up his cell phone and jiggled it at her—a reminder to call if she needed him. Then walked away. Yet as he walked he stopped when a little boy ran up to him, holding out his *boina* for pesos. He gave the child a handful of money and tousled his hair, which made her picture of Jack even more confusing. "I don't think I'm wrong about you, Jack Kenner," she whispered. Surprisingly, he was still carrying his lights in her last image of him before he faded into the darkness.

The hospital was unusually quiet. Most of the patients had checked themselves out to go to the festival, and it was almost eerie wandering down the hall, hearing nothing but the echo of his own footsteps on the cement floors. So maybe being alone wasn't everything it was cracked up to be. He was used to it, though. It was what he knew, what he did. His comfort zone. But should he have stayed, tried putting on the pretense of fun for Amanda? She did try hard, and her intentions were so...so selfless. In fact, he couldn't remember ever knowing someone as selfless as she was. That, plus the village did put on a nice party.

Nice village, nice party, nice people... There'd been a time when he'd thought about raising Rosa in as much of her heritage as he could, and the festivals were part of that. Something he'd looked forward to for a little while. He'd pictured her in party dresses, with flowers in her hair. Dancing, playing...having fun. Pictured her older, too, with the little boys beginning to take notice, even though she was still clinging to her daddy's hand. Then pictured her even beyond that, when the boys grew up and he held on tighter.

Pointless memories that had never happened. A

miserable reminder of his failings, and Rosa had never got to go to her parties or festivals.

Trying to blot out everything but the sound of his footsteps, Jack cleared his throat as he approached Ezequiel's room. "You in here?" he asked, pushing open the door. No answer, and no Ezequiel. He was probably in town, admiring the lights like everybody else. Which made this the perfect time...

Jack looked up and down the hall, saw no one anywhere, and crept into Ezequiel's room, shutting the door behind him. The boy didn't have much. Some books, precious few clothes, the water bottle, which sat prominently on a shelf. And a framed photo of a woman—young, vital, with Ezequiel's smile. Ezequiel's mother, Jack guessed, a lump forming in his throat. The boy had so little in the world, yet he didn't know that because he was happy. And optimistic. He was grateful for what he had rather than resentful for all those things he didn't have. There was a lesson to be learned there, Jack thought as he tossed the boxes of lights on the cot Ezequiel used as a bed and got to work.

Okay, so maybe he wasn't quite the grump he let on he was. The kid deserved something nice in his life, and while lights were only a temporary bandage on a much bigger hurt, sometimes a bandage helped. So Jack set about the chore, stringing lights over the two-drawer stand, the clothes rod hanging above the bed, the shelf, the door. If there was a place to string lights, he did, and when he left the closet-size area a little while later, purposely leaving the lights on so Ezequiel would see the effect the instant he opened his door, Jack was pleased. And melancholy. It wasn't much, not nearly as much as the kid deserved, but Ezequiel didn't measure his life in terms of what was much, or what he deserved. Jack vowed, though, that next time he went to the village he'd buy a couple of trinkets for Ezequiel, and wrap them for Christmas. He himself wouldn't still be here then, he hoped, but every kid needed a present or two.

Walking across the compound, where a mischievous light fairy had stopped and strung a few strands of lights, Jack thought back to Christmas mornings with Robbie, remembered his brother's excitement, not so much over what he got as the fact that he had presents to unwrap. It hadn't mattered to Robbie that they were all wrapped alike, or that there was a uniform consistency to them. It hadn't mattered that the decorations and lights on the tree were all one color, and every ornament was a precisely measured distance from the one next to it. No, none of that made a difference because his brother had looked at it with such innocence. And awe. In all those Christmases Jack had hated, Robbie had found so much joy and wonderment.

Jack missed that innocence, ached to have it back sometimes. But nothing in his life was innocent. He'd traveled too far, seen too many things, felt the pain of the ultimate failure. So there was no innocence left for him.

Except…Ezequiel. He still had that innocence, that honest expectation of life that everything worked out. For the boy's sake, he hoped Ezequiel could keep that for a long, long time.

Hoped that he would find joy and wonderment in a simple string of lights.

So, now what? More journals? Read until he fell asleep? Stare up at the ceiling until the monotony dulled his senses enough to empty his head of the thoughts that usually kept him awake half the night? Go prowl the hospital, see if anything there clicked as a cause of the outbreak? Didn't matter. None of it did because that was the normal cycle of his life, the things he did out of habit. Had done before, would do again no matter where he was. Except tonight the music from the festival wafted over the hospital, and he could hear bursts of muffled laughter from the village. Some of it probably Amanda's.

Amanda... He had to stop doing this to himself. Stop torturing himself. Because what the hell good did it do, thinking about her when that was as far as it could ever go? He'd successfully gone maybe ten minutes without thinking about her, but there she was, right back in his head. He couldn't let her stay there, fought to get her out because why let her stay when the result would be something he couldn't hang on to?

But she was there again, like it or not, and as he trudged up the wooden steps to the guest hut, her name pounded rhythmically into his brain the way his feet pounded their rhythm on the wooden planks. *Amanda... Amanda...* "What the...?"

"Surprise!" she said, flipping the light switch that lit up the lights strung around his bed the instant he stepped through the door.

"This is payback, right? I left the festival before my two hours were up so you're paying me back by trying to electrocute me with Christmas lights?"

"Yep, Jack. That's exactly what I'm trying to do—electrocute you." Laughing, she circled around behind him then handed him an *alfajores de maizena*—starch cookie, along with a cup of thick juice. "Mango and orange," she said. "Since you wouldn't stay at the party, I brought the party to you."

"Lights on my bed is a party?" he asked, trying to hold back even though he was touched by her effort.

"It's also a thank-you for being honest with me earlier. Knowing where I might be from is very important to me, Jack. It doesn't answer all the millions of questions I've had for most of my life, but it's a start, and it's more than I had. So I'm grateful, and I'm also sorry if the way I pushed you into telling me caused you any conflict or concern, as that wasn't my intention. But I'm glad I did, because you told me something I needed more than you can know."

She walked over to him, stood on her tiptoes and kissed him on the cheek. "That's for being honest with me."

An honesty that already plagued him, as Amanda was building up hopes that could break her heart. It was not what he wanted and not what he'd intended to do. He might be wrong, but he was pretty certain that she was Mapuche, and how could he have lied to her about that? In truth, he couldn't. Still, her knowledge wasn't necessarily going to be kind and that, more than anything, was his regret. "I was afraid I might owe you an apology for butting in. It wasn't any of my business."

"Except you didn't butt in. I dragged you, and I would have kept after you until you told me. I saw it in you, Jack. Your eyes don't lie. When you looked at me…maybe not *at* me as much as past, me…you knew. Or maybe that was wishful thinking. Whatever the case, the truth is the truth. It scares me but I'll deal with it."

Naive assertion, he thought. The truth could be the most painful thing any person ever had to bear. That was what he knew on the deepest level, because the pain of his truths never left him. For Amanda, though, he was glad her naivety served as a shield. He only hoped it was strong enough to sustain her. "Well, I'm sorry, anyway. If not for any offenses I've already created, then I'm sure there'll be a few in my future. So, hold that apology on account, will you?"

"That sure of yourself?" she asked, breaking a pinch off the cookie he wasn't eating and popping it into her mouth. "Um," she murmured apprecia-tively, going back for a second pinch.

"Years and years of experience."

"And years and years…" she continued, look-ing up at him with wide eyes,

"Not that many," he grumbled, handing her his cookie.

"You sure?" she teased.

"Okay, well, maybe that many. I do have my reputation…"

"Hard earned and well deserved…or not." She broke the cookie into two pieces then handed half back to him. "So, earlier, when you said there was a woman, someone Mapuche…"

Just like that, all the niceness switched off for him. One little reminder and he was thrown back into the past. He struggled against it, for Amanda. She didn't need that image, that ugliness touch-ing her. No one did.

"Like I said, I lived in the region for a while. Went there to chase down a contaminant in an orphanage, and decided to stay because…because I liked the area. Got to know the people, became familiar with the Mapuche subtleties. Like your skin color, and the sculpture of your cheekbones. It's very characteristic, very…" He closed his eyes, pictured Rosa. Fought back the lump forming in his throat. "Very nice. When you travel as extensively as I do, chasing after the things I chase, you become good at observing everything around you."

"Did you fall in love there?" she asked. "When you were out in the Pampas villages, did you fall in love with someone?"

He shook his head. "There was this woman…. She caught my eye for a moment, but it didn't work out. Two different worlds. She didn't want to leave hers, I didn't want to leave mine. No, I didn't fall in love. Maybe got a little wiser…" What the hell was he doing, talking about this, talking about anything coming from that part of his life? And how was it that Amanda made it so easy for him to simply start rambling like he was, when that part of his life was off-limits to everyone?

She was getting too close, that was how it was. And he was letting her. Damn, he had to get a better grip. And fast. "Have you told Ben yet?" he asked, making an abrupt change in the subject.

"That I think I'm Mapuche? Not sure how I'm going to do that without implying our parents were…" She shrugged. "Tomorrow, though. And on that note, it's been a long day. For both of us. So I'm going to pull the dividing curtain and bid you happy dreams. And, Jack…really, thank you."

Even with a curtain dividing them, he wasn't sure he could sleep. Too many things had him wound up. Amanda, Rosa, Robbie. Even Ezequiel. "Think I'll go find a rocker out on the porch and read for a while," he said, grabbing his journal and heading for the door. Once there, he turned, only to find Amanda standing in the middle of the room, curtain half-pulled across, merely staring at him. After the longest half minute in the history of the world, she finally pulled the curtain the rest of the way shut, and only her silhouette shone through. "Enjoy the Christmas lights, Jack," she called.

CHAPTER FOUR

"I THOUGHT you might like a cup of tea," Amanda whispered, trying not to break the silence in the dark of the room. Jack was seated at the desk at the edge of the children's ward, keeping himself to the shadows and simply staring at...well, she wasn't sure. Standing out in the hall, she'd watched him through the door window for a few moments. He'd barely moved. But for the rise and fall of his chest outlined in silhouette, he might have been a statue or a cardboard cutout of a guardian angel sitting there, looking over the children. "It's plain. None of the local spices."

"Thank you," he said, without stirring to take the cup from her.

So she set it down, took a step backward. Thought about leaving, but didn't. "What are you looking for?" she finally asked. He hadn't ever come back into the guest hut. She'd stayed awake a little while, listening for him then had finally drifted off. Later, when the that vexing little howler monkey who lived in the jungle canopy outside had decided to wake up and exercise his air-raid-loud call, probably in the hope of finding a girlfriend who, mercifully, didn't howl, she'd got up to shut the window and seen he still wasn't there.

"Don't know exactly."

"Then why are you here?"

"Sometimes I find the answers I need in the observations. Doing all the tests is fine, but too often the human element is left out of the diagnosis, and that's unfortunate because as doctors we need to stay involved. So while I don't actively treat the patients too often, I like to observe them." Finally, he budged. He looked up at her then drew in a deep breath. "What I observed tonight is that the girl, third bed on the right, has an elevated temperature…to the touch. It's not appreciable; I didn't take a reading with a thermometer. But by morning it will register enough for us to be concerned. That, and she's listless…something there's no test for, but it's a real symptom. Then another child, the boy, last bed on the far side, is more restless than he was earlier. Started about fifteen minutes ago with him kicking off his sheets, and I'm thinking he's getting ready to have a stomachache as he's curling up on his side." He took a sip of the tea. "So why are you here?"

"Monkey outside my window woke me up."

He chuckled. "You know those howlers are the loudest animal in the world, don't you?"

"Especially when he's looking for his lady love."

"Poor guy's probably frustrated as hell." He took another sip. "Can't blame him for trying, though I'd think all that bellowing would drive her away."

"Or make her fall madly in love if he's bellowing to his soul mate." Jack bellowed, she thought. Did he do it to drive people away from him? "So, we've got two more kids getting sick. What are we going to do?"

Jack shrugged. "Even though this bug is probably not communicable by proximity, we separate them from the rest of the kids in the ward. It's easier to watch for specific symptoms that way."

"Which isn't going to be easy as we don't have an abundance of extra rooms. But I'll see what I can find. What's your guess, by the way? I'm assuming you have some idea of what we're dealing with."

"Maybe. But it's something I always keep to myself until I know more. People panic, Amanda. They hear a word, get all kinds of ideas, do all kinds of crazy things. I learned a long time ago that while I'm at the guessing stage, it's better to keep it to myself."

"Makes sense," she said. "Except to the part-owner of the hospital. And she's pretty anxious to know *anything,* even a guess."

"So you're pulling rank on me, turning into my boss?"

Amanda laughed. "Has anybody ever truly been your boss, Jack?"

Smiling, he said, "Once, when I was a kid, I worked in this fast-food restaurant… Actually, I think I caused my boss to quit his job. As in turned in his paper hat in the middle of the shift and ran out the door."

"Because?"

"Kitchen was filthy. I called the Board of Health from his office phone, right in front of him. Probably called him out by name, although I don't remember that part. But it sounds like something I'd do, doesn't it?"

"Probably. But for the greater good, I think. At least, I hope it wasn't over some burnt burgers."

"Burnt would have been preferable. In my mind, I remember the hamburger meat having a greenish tint to it."

Amanda turned up her nose. "So, you've been chasing contaminants of some sort since you were a boy."

"That was my first time. Didn't really know much about contaminants except that green meat probably had something bad growing in it."

"So, what's growing here, Jack? Give me some idea, or at least some hope."

"Hope comes when I nail the diagnosis, because I've never faced anything yet that can't be cured.

And this can be cured, Amanda, because the symptoms seem like they're water-borne. Haven't figured out how, but I do have a few culprits in mind, and that's all I'm going to say except that I don't want to move these kids until we know their room is as sterile as we can make it, even though I doubt the bug is growing outside a water source.

"But better safe than sorry. So, after we get them settled in, I'll want cultures of blood, urine, sputum, and other bodily fluids, as well as wound cultures if they have any open incisions, cuts, scrapes or lesions. I'd also like to get some general skin scrapings, just to see what's growing on the surface, because I'm tired of waiting and while I'm leaning in one direction based on a hunch, I need a definitive answer on if we're dealing with a bacterium, a fungal infection, a virus, or some other kind of microorganism…in the event I'm wrong."

"All this without getting any sleep?"

"I slept. Dozed in the chair on the porch for an hour or two."

Rather than sleeping on the other side of the

curtain. She didn't know what to make of it. Felt a little hurt, maybe a little angry. But it shouldn't matter because he was doing exactly what he was supposed to be doing—solving the problem. So it was her hurt and anger to get rid of, or allow to bother her. Either way, it had nothing to do with Jack and everything to do with her.

Still, she'd liked that idea that he would be sleeping on the other side of the curtain. It made her feel…less vulnerable. So much for that, though. "By your own admission, you never get it wrong. At least, that's what you told me earlier today…actually, that would be yesterday now, wouldn't it?"

"About my *bugs,* as I call them?" He shook his head. "No, I don't get it wrong because in due course those are the easy things to deal with. They have a pattern, they make logical sense as they're wreaking their havoc. It's life in general I get wrong, pretty much on a daily basis because there's nothing logical about it. Nothing to make sense of out of the havoc it wreaks."

"Maybe if you think of life in terms of something that doesn't need to be fixed or cured so much as something that needs to be enjoyed, you'd be able to deal with it better."

"Easy for the optimist to say."

"I'm not an optimist, Jack. But I'm practical, and practicality in my life dictates I'm happier when I enjoy life, which in turn makes me a better person, which makes me a better doctor. It all works together."

"But practicality in my life is about the work, and the means to an end for whatever I'm trying to find. I don't need to enjoy it, and fixing or curing it isn't hinged on anything other than one goal, which is to stop the contaminant. No joy in it, nothing to make me a better person. Just a matter of something that needs to be dealt with."

"No pride in your accomplishment?"

"Sometimes. I mean, I do have some ego invested. But pride isn't the same thing as joy. Joy comes from another place.... A place I don't need to access."

"Then it's your loss."

"How can you lose something you've never had? Anyway, once I get the contaminant identified, I want to test it for its sensitivity to a range of drugs so that each child can be treated as quickly and as effectively as we're able to do with an appropriate medicine. Then in the meantime, while we're waiting for test results, I'd like to start preventative treatment with a broad-spectrum antibiotic such as penicillin. It's probably not necessary, but I don't want anything else creeping up on us."

"Poor Jack. All work, no play makes him a curmudgeon." But a very sexy one. And she wanted to be the one to break through the rocky exterior because underneath she knew she'd find something else entirely. Maybe something smoldering, or about to erupt. Maybe just a little joy waiting to happen, but not knowing how to do it.

"All work and no play saves lives." He shifted in his chair then stood. "So right now this curmudgeon is going to take himself to the pharmacy to see what antibiotics are available for prophylactic treatment."

Amanda laughed. "Now I get it. First you prescribe then you keep your fingers crossed."

He chuckled. "Something like that." Stepping

away from the desk, he motioned for Amanda to follow him into the hall. "Don't want to wake the kids," he said, shutting the door behind him but turning his back to her so he could watch through the window to the ward. "I also want this ward disinfected once we get the kids separated. I know it's been cleaned, probably several times, but I don't want anything left behind."

"You're talking about a lot of resources, Jack. We'll do the best we can, but I can't make any promises. I mean, have you even looked at this place? We operate on nothing. We get expired drugs to give to our patients…. They're still good, still usable, but because they're past their date they can't be sold on the open market, which makes them affordable for us. Also, some of the pharmacies donate them to us, and we have to make use of prescriptions patients turn back in to us because they didn't take all the pills.

"We have used beds, used equipment, limited space. The cost of a single X-ray almost breaks our back, and if it weren't for the kindness of the village women who, as a courtesy, launder our sheets and blankets at their homes, I don't even know how we'd manage doing all that. Food is donated, most of our workers are volunteers. Villagers, who barely have enough to support their own families, leave coins and food on our doorstep to help keep us going.

"So we'll do everything we can to give you what you need. But be patient with us. It takes time. Sometimes it takes begging."

She appreciated his dedication, but appreciating it and knowing what to do about it were two entirely separate things and she was beginning to wonder if Jack was the kind of man who would pick up and leave if he didn't get everything he wanted, when he wanted it. The Jack Kenner she wanted him to be wouldn't, but the Jack Kenner she had standing in front of her right now, the one with expectations they couldn't even begin to fulfill—she didn't know how this was going to work.

"Begging," he grunted. "Fat lot of good that ever does. Especially when people hear only what they want to hear or see only what they want to see."

"Spoken like a man who knows."

"Spoken like a man who won't beg."

"Something from your childhood?" she asked, wondering about the bitterness he wasn't even trying to hide.

"Something from my entire life," he snapped.

See, that was just the way he was. Bordering on friendly one minute, shoving her away the next. It was frustrating. More than that, she was beginning to wonder why she even cared, why she even gave him a thought outside what she'd brought him here to do. It was clear Jack didn't want to be sociable, so why bother?

"Look, on that *sour* note, I'm going to go take my morning shower, then get started on the things you need. If you think of something else…" She shut her eyes, angrier at herself for reacting to his abrupt attitude change than at him for doing such a fast turnaround, nice to contentious in the blink of an eye. "Write it down and tack it to my office door." That said, Amanda spun away and walked down the hall, concentrating on each step she took, measuring her rhythm, keeping it even. Unlike her heart, which was beating erratically.

"I didn't mean to do that," he said, catching up to her and grabbing hold of her arm to slow her down.

"Hey, I'm not the one who's always at odds with the world." She stopped, looked up at him. "But you are, Jack. It's your business, and I'm not going to ask you what's going on because I refuse to turn this into an analyst-patient situation. Not with you. But let me warn you, *as a friend,* it's going to eat you up until there's nothing left. You can't go on living your life the way you do without hurting yourself. In your case, though, since you don't seem to care about yourself..."

"What do you want to hear? That my general loathing of all things happy and fun started in my childhood? Would it make you feel better knowing that I didn't grow up in the loving adopted family you did? That my father's wife, Cade's mother, by the way, adopted me for appearances, and we were forevermore a dysfunctional family of haters and malcontents. Except for Robbie, who was the only good thing..." He stopped, bit down hard on his lip.

"It wouldn't make me feel better knowing any of that, Jack, because I'm not the one who goes around with a perpetual scowl on my face and acid in my belly. But if telling me makes you feel better, then tell me."

"Always the shrink, aren't you?"

"No, Jack. Always the friend. I'm sorry you don't know the difference." More than that, she was sorry she couldn't make a difference for Jack because he had so much good locked away inside. She'd seen it as she'd watched him watch the children a little while ago. Too bad the Jack Kenner standing there frowning at her right now couldn't get to know *that* Jack Kenner. Odds were if he did, he probably wouldn't like him very much. She did, though. She liked *that* Jack Kenner more than she wanted to. Funny thing was, she liked this one, too. Go figure.

"It was like a miracle!" Ezequiel exclaimed. "I opened the door and they weren't there, then all of a sudden my room… It was full of lights."

"What kind of lights?" Amanda asked, knowing

exactly where they'd come from. But it wasn't a miracle. It had been Jack, and it was exactly what he would do. Three strands of lights for one little boy and her heart swelled just a little. One minute she was ready to forget Jack existed, then the next minute she was practically weepy over something sweet he'd done for Ezequiel.

"All colors, like the lights in the village."

"And you're sure they weren't there when you left to go to festival?"

Ezequiel shook his head. "Just the one on the ceiling."

"Then I think it's a miracle!" she exclaimed, handing him a box of cotton swabs to carry from the storeroom to the ward. "And I'd like to come and see it later on, if you don't mind. You, um… You didn't mention this to Dr. Kenner, did you?"

"You mean Doc K?" He shook his head. "He had a hundred people in line to see him this morning. He didn't have time."

Jack was handling outpatient clinic this morning? He was certainly full of surprises. "Look, you take those swabs and give them to Nurse Consuela, and I think I'll go see if Jack…Doc K needs some help with those hundred patients."

One hundred turned out to be an exaggeration, but the dozen standing in line waiting for Jack's attention were glad to see her. So was Jack, who'd just finished examining a long-standing case of dry hacks from one of the village's most notorious smokers. "He thought I might have something your brother hasn't suggested," Jack said as Amanda entered the tiny office where Jack was washing his hands and getting ready to see his next patient.

"Did you?" she asked, fighting back a smile.

He nodded toward the trash can, where an almost full pack of *cigarillos* had been discarded, all wadded up.

"Do you know how much those cost him?" she asked, impressed he'd had the nerve to do what needed to be done, even though that wouldn't make him any friends here.

"Do you know how much of my time he wasted when he's not willing to make an effort to quit?"

"Señor Juarez sits on the village governing

board. He's not really a good friend to the hospital. Doesn't like outsiders interfering with the people here. But it's a relationship my brother's been trying to cultivate, so I hope you didn't do something to…"

"Consider it cultivated." A slow, amused smile spread across his face. "Better than cultivated, actually. More like rock solid."

"How, when you threw away his *cigarillos?* He loves those things, Jack. Would sooner give up his wife than his smokes. And he's got a lovely wife."

"I mentioned the wheezes in his chest. It caught his interest."

"He was wheezing?"

"A little. Nothing I'd consider serious. But I did say how wheezes could be an early warning of other lung disease—asthma, emphysema. Maybe I might have mentioned something about a lifetime of inhalers and oxygen. And that I couldn't make a proper diagnosis because I didn't have the right equipment."

"Am I going to regret the end of the story, where

Señor Juarez vows to shut down the hospital if it's the last thing he ever does?"

"Oh, ye of little faith."

"Oh, me with lots of prior experience with the man."

"Well, in this case, *new* experience paid off because I think you'll prefer the ending where Señor Juarez promises to scrounge every hospital in Argentina if that's what it takes to find us some used pulmonary function testing equipment."

"Seriously? He's going to help us?"

He kept a deliberately stoic face. "And here you were, thinking the worst of me."

"Does he have some kind of chronic obstructive pulmonary disease?" she asked.

Jack shook his head. "Probably not. I prescribed some antibiotics for a mild case of bronchitis, though. With the promise that Señor Juarez will be the first one tested on our new equipment, once he finds it."

"You're bad," she said, smiling. Another one of those near-weepy moments.

"Been accused of worse."

"Do you ever just try to make things easy?"

"You mean, on purpose?" he asked, giving way to a half smile.

"Maybe not," she said. "Because sometimes bad is very, *very* good, isn't it?"

He felt the zing of her words, the heat and tension of them. Had to take in a deep breath to steady himself. Another time, another place, he and Amanda might have had a different ending to *their* story. Too bad he'd slipped ahead to the end of the book and knew what was there. Too damn bad.

"Anyway, I'm here to relieve you so you can get back to what you'd rather be doing. We turned the waiting room into your isolation room, moved the waiting room to the front porch, and I've got several people ready to start cleaning as soon as you give the word. So you'd better go take charge."

"What about the rest of my patients here? I can't just walk away and leave them."

"I'll make sure they're seen. Oh, and, Jack, those lights in Ezequiel's room…"

"What lights?" he asked, jotting down a quick note in a patient chart then snapping it shut.

"The Christmas lights."

"The kid strung up some Christmas lights? Good for him."

"You're not very good at acting innocent, you know."

"Innocent of what?"

"He thinks it was a miracle, Jack. One minute they weren't there, then the next they were."

"Lights are lights. Let the kid believe whatever he wants to believe. It doesn't really matter, does it?"

"Yes, it matters," she said, stepping up to him, standing on tiptoe and kissing him on the cheek. "It matters because it was a nice thing you did for him. In a more devious way, a nice thing you did for Señor Juarez, too. And the hospital, as we're going to get some equipment. Nice, all the way around."

Niceties made him nervous. They came with motives and obligations, and he'd given all that up years ago. "You're not going to kiss me again, are you?" he asked, laying his hand on doorknob, hesitating because he was actually hoping for what was turning into her customary thank-you.

"Maybe I won't..." She smiled and stepped up to him. "Maybe I will." This time, though, the kiss wasn't to his cheek. It was full on the lips. Not a brush to his lips, though, or lingering. More like a promise. And by the time he was out in the hall, his knees were shaking. Well, maybe not so much in the literal sense as the figurative, but he did stop, raise his fingers to his lips, and wonder.

"What the hell are you doing, Kenner?" he asked himself, quite aware there wasn't a rational answer in him when it came to Amanda. "What the hell are you doing?"

"You're setting up a new ward?" Ben called from halfway down the hall. He was emerging from a patient room, working at twice the speed of anybody else at the hospital, looking worn out even though the day had barely begun.

Did the man ever sleep? Jack wondered, because from the look of him he seemed like someone who would prowl the halls eternally. But everybody had their own way to avoid whatever it was they wanted to avoid. Life, people, love…that void where something you cared for was ripped away.

Jack had developed several means of turning away from what he didn't want to see, and he practiced them with the skill of a master. Not gladly, but necessarily. And he was sure Ben would share that same deep understanding. He saw it in the lines etched on Ben's face. "We need to get the kids isolated, not so much because of what they have but because I want to keep them restricted from what other people might give them. So I've got it in the works right now. Amanda turned over the waiting room to me."

Ben nodded his approval. "As you've noticed by now, I'm not much of a manager. So I appreciate you taking charge of this and moving forward."

"You manage in subtleties. Pretty smart and, as Amanda accused me of being, pretty devious."

"Yes, the pulmonary-function equipment. Good job, turning Señor Juarez around not only in our favor but sending him out to scrounge equipment.

If you knew how many times I've tried to get that man to cut back on his smoking… Anyway, back to the bug."

"The bug… I made some calls. A few people owe me favors, and I've called some of them in. If you can find me the transport, I can get the testing supplies we need."

"Should I bother asking how?"

"Nothing illegal. And contrary to what your sister might think, nothing even devious. But when you travel as much as I have, you meet people, do some favors. People make promises. You know, *If you ever need anything…* I happen to be one of those who hangs on to those promises, because you never know when you'll need to call one in." Jack held up his cell phone. "I called. Now I have to work out the logistics of getting the supplies flown in."

"Amanda said you were different. She sure as hell was right about that."

"Have you talked to her since last night?"

Ben nodded. "Briefly."

"She told you what I said to her?"

"About her potentially being Mapuche? You know, I really don't have time to get into it now, but how could you do that? Without proof, *why* would you do that?"

Jack chuckled humorlessly. "She asked, I answered. But you already knew, or suspected, didn't you, Ben? You know the people. You know the differences between someone from a Mediterranean background and someone from the Pampas regions in Argentina."

"What I know… All I know is that our parents found life easier by taking the path of least resistance. Not searching for my sister's heritage made life easier for them."

"But you knew she wanted to know and yet you didn't tell her."

"Tell her what? Because I don't *know* anything. Neither do you. So why drag her through that when there's nothing to be gained?"

"There comes a point, Ben, when protection turns into suffocation. Then everybody involved gets hurt. But that's for you and your sister to sort out." He patted Ben on the shoulder. "I shouldn't have been the one to tell her, but I wasn't going to be the one to lie. She's strong, though. She'll work through it." He got why Ben was angry. What he didn't get, though, was why he'd kept the secret. Protecting parents was one thing, but weighing that against Amanda's right to know? Well, it was between Ben and his sister now. He hoped they could, or would, work it out. "Anyway, after I get the supplies we need lined up…"

"I'll call in a favor or two of my own. You do what you have to, and I'll make arrangements for a plane."

"Seriously?" Even though Amanda had un-knowingly pitted him against Ben, he liked the guy. He was smart and resourceful. And being a devoted brother wasn't the worst thing in the world. Too bad he and Ben had absurdly differ-ent views on Amanda's well-being, or else they might have become friends.

"As serious as I am about protecting my sister."

So there it was, the implied threat. Except it was unnecessary. He wasn't the one who *would* hurt her, or *had* hurt her. "I'm not going to hurt

Amanda, Ben. But I'm not going to protect her to her detriment, either."

Ben nodded, but didn't respond. Rather, he turned and walked away, not even glancing back when he rounded the corner.

Amanda stepped up behind Jack yet kept a proper distance. "He's always tried to take care of me, almost from the first day my parents brought me home. I was a toddler, and Ben just swooped in and hasn't ever really swooped out. That's what makes him such a good doctor. He truly cares."

"So why Argentina?"

"What do you mean?"

"Why is he operating this hospital in Argentina? He could have gone to Peru or Brazil, could have gone to any number of places in Africa, but he's here, and you have a heritage here."

"Coincidence?" she asked.

"Could be," Jack said, moving on past her. "Have you ever asked him why he came to Argentina?" There was so much protectiveness going on between brother and sister, yet Jack wondered what happened when you broke through that layer.

There was definitely something else happening underneath, some kind of a riptide waiting to swell up and pull someone under. So, what was it? Ben hadn't admitted he knew Amanda was Mapuche, but what if he did? What if he *did* know, and…

Damn. Suddenly, it hit him. So obvious, so unthinkable. The beginnings of a truth that might be better off unanswered if he intended to keep his promise to Ben. He wouldn't hurt Amanda. *Wouldn't.* Not for any reason. Still, her Mapuche heritage… Ben suspected. He suspected the same thing Jack did. *Damn it to hell.* Why had she asked him—him of all people—who she was? And why couldn't he have simply left it alone? Stuck to his tried and true life course and kept his distance?

Because she was Amanda, that was why. Persuasive. Impossible to resist. Impossible for *him* to resist. Amanda.

A sudden, cold chill ran up Jack's spine. Not one that tingled but one that jabbed hard. *What have I done?* She was too inquisitive, she would want to know the answer to the question he'd posed: Why Argentina? She'd ask until she found out, and that was what he berated himself with over and over as his thoughts came together and his suspicions locked into place like pieces of a jigsaw puzzle. Pieces of Amanda.

What have I done?

He'd opened a door—that was what. Now he sincerely regretted that she wasn't Mediterranean. Wished he hadn't recognized the Mapuche in her.

On the other hand, maybe he was wrong about everything. Maybe Rosa's tragedy had jaded his life so badly he couldn't see anything through the haze except more heartache. *God, please, let it be faulty judgment.* It wasn't much of a hope to hang anything on. It was all he had, though. The hope he was wrong.

Somehow, however, he knew he wasn't. When that realization punched him, another cold chill shot up his spine, and this one settled in. What the hell had he done to Amanda?

"This is the last bed, Doc," Ezequiel called to him thirty minutes later. He'd been serving as translator throughout the whole cleaning process. "All clean. Ready for sheets."

Without real testing equipment, there wasn't much he could do. He still had a few swabs left, and some culture dishes not yet contaminated. It didn't come close to being enough, but it would work for now. On the bright side, the room was sanitized thanks to the generous efforts of village volunteers. Not sterilized, but as clean as it could be under the circumstances, and every one of the ladies who'd trooped in earlier with mops and pails had put their hearts and souls into the chore.

"Tell the ladies to go ahead and make up the beds," he instructed Ezequiel, as he climbed out from under one of the beds he'd been swabbing and stood up. "Oh, and after we get this transfer made, I'd like to see your lights."

"You would?" Ezequiel cried.

Jack forced a smile, even though he didn't feel much like smiling. His mind was still on Amanda, what he'd said, what he might have set in motion by telling her who she might be. "I want to see how they're strung, because I'm thinking about putting lights in here."

"All the rooms?" Ezequiel asked. "Could we put them in all the rooms? I can do that, Doc K. Please, let me be the one."

"You're not really allowed to go in the patient rooms, are you?"

Ezequiel's face dropped. "No, Doc Ben won't let me."

Jack fished a handful of money from his pocket and gave it to the boy. "Well, we're just going to have to figure where those lights will go, won't we? But first go down to the village and see how many you can buy."

"With all the money?" he asked, the excitement starting to return.

"All the money. Oh, and, Ezequiel…" He handed the boy a few more bills. "Stop and buy some empanadas from one of the vendors, and some of that *mate* tea. Enough for everybody who's volunteering this morning." He thought about the boy trying to lug all that back then had second thoughts. "Actually, you go get the lights, I'll get the food." Which was what he did. Trotted straight out the door, then halfway to the village Amanda caught up to him.

"I hear we're going to have a party this afternoon. That's so nice of you, Jack. I love parties, especially when they're impromptu."

He clenched his jaw when he saw her. In the past little while he'd reasoned himself out of believing that she would ask the Argentina question. He hoped she would, didn't know what he'd do if she didn't. Then come back to the one sure thing he knew above all else—Amanda was strong. If his mention of Ben's motives for being in Argentina opened up doors she found difficult, he'd help her shut them or move through them. He'd created the rift, and that was all he could do to make amends.

In all likelihood she was a child of Argentina, and wasn't it her right to know for sure? And it wasn't like she hadn't already been looking for herself. Still... "We're going to have food as in feed the volunteers for working so hard."

"Food and lights and tea. To some, that's a party, Jack."

"Let me guess. You're one of those people who believes everything can be a party?"

"It can, if you want it to be. It's all in your attitude."

"Then it's a good thing mine is perpetually bad, or else I might be partying every day."

Amanda laughed. "Your true colors are showing, Jack."

"You mean my evil, dark heart?" A heart that couldn't quite achieve any shade of dark when it came to Amanda.

"I mean whatever you're trying to hide isn't hidden very well. Lights, tea, empanadas..." Grinning, Amanda latched on to his arm. "Oh, and to go with the empanadas and tea, I'd think about buying something sweet. A pastry. Maybe some *facturas.* And just so you'll know, the best ones are stuffed with *crema pastelera, dulce de leche* or *membrillo,* then sprinkled with sugar or icing. Try the *panaderia* on the last corner on the left. Theirs are the best. So, now that I've fulfilled my mission in convincing you to buy *facturas,* see you back at the hospital." She unlatched her arm from his, and stepped away.

"You think I'm convinced?"

She wrinkled her nose. "I know you're convinced."

"But you're not going with me to make sure?" he asked, admittedly disappointed. The feel of her hanging on to him was actually quite pleasant. They'd been a nice few steps with her, and he'd hoped for a few more.

She shook her head. "I'm going to do a quick physical on each of the kids we're moving before we get them settled in. I know you checked them last night, but I want to see if anything's changed. By the time you get back, we should be well under way with the transfer."

"So you chased after me halfway to the village because…"

"Because I like *facturas.* And in case you're interested, *dulce de leche* is my favorite."

She smiled, spun around and headed straight back to the hospital. And Jack watched, couldn't help himself. Today, her shorts were more modest, her shirt a simple, oversized gauzy cotton, her hair tied up more the way he was used to seeing it. All of it so…sexy. Which was why he watched. Couldn't have helped himself if he'd wanted to. He didn't want to.

"All of them, Doc K," Ezequiel shouted, from the other side of the street.

The boy's voice broke though Jack's distraction, and he blinked hard to refocus. "What?"

"The lights. I bought all of them." His arms were stacked with boxes of lights, almost more than he could juggle. "We can light up the whole hospital."

Jack's mind wasn't on lighting up the whole hospital. It was on one bed only, already strung with lights, and the curtain that separated it from the bed across the room. Such an imposing piece of thin cloth, and while it wasn't yet noon he was already preparing himself to lose sleep over it tonight.

Had to be a bug bite, he thought as he headed for the *panaderia,* hoping for *dulce de leche.* Some uncharted bug must have bitten him and sucked out all his common sense. That was all it could be. Yep, definitely all it could be.

CHAPTER FIVE

"DAY after tomorrow?" Jack asked, steadying his thin thread of forbearance with a calming breath. The delay was nobody's fault. He understood that. Testing supplies were en route, but their free plane ride had been delayed a day while the plane was being serviced. Now all he could do was sit and twiddle his thumbs and at the same time try to keep up a facade of patience. Neither twiddling nor patience were his strong suits. But he didn't want Amanda to see his ruffled feathers because... Well, it mattered. He didn't know why, as he'd never really tried creating a good impression before. Accept him or not. Either way, it didn't matter because he got along with his life just fine, no muss, no fuss.

So this was quite an unexpected turn for him, trying to make a good impression. And he wasn't very adept at it. He felt that hot bother creeping along the edges of his collar, considered opening the window and just jumping out. "If that's the best they can do, it'll be fine. We'll make it work until then." Said with a clenched jaw.

Ben shrugged. "Wish I had better news for you."

"Me, too, since this morning we had our first adult patient come down with mild symptoms, and I'm betting there will be more to follow." Jack wedged himself between Ben and Ben's desk, trying to avoid the scent he knew had to be Amanda's shampoo. The quarters here were abysmally tight, and all three of them were nearly pressed together in this little conference. He didn't like anybody in his personal space, and he didn't like being in anybody else's personal space. Yet here he was, personal space overlapping all over the place, especially with Amanda, where the scent of her was reminding him of things he didn't get to have.

He needed room, air to breathe. Needed Amanda a safe distance away from him. But this spur-of-the-moment meeting had to be here, shoulder to shoulder, because Jack feared being overheard anywhere else. One misunderstood word turned into misconceptions, turned into panic. He'd seen it happen before. Seen all hell break loose. People getting scared. Out of control. Doing crazy things because they didn't understand.

That was what had happened with Rosa, why she'd died—misconceptions and panic. People who hadn't understood and conditions too chaotic to listen. So now better cramped than sorry.

Never mind he wanted to bury his face in Amanda's hair and nuzzle. "Like I told Amanda, I could take an educated guess what we're dealing with because I'm pretty sure it's some sort of waterborne problem. Depending on which one it is, the treatment would be vastly different, though."

"We're talking about what kind of life form?" Ben asked. "Protozoan, viral, bacterial, parasites?"

"Take your pick. The symptoms are all similar, with some distinctions, and right now I'm looking for those distinctions."

"And apart from the preventative antibiotics

you're prescribing, is there anything else we can do?" Amanda asked.

"Treat symptoms like you've already been doing. Antinausea drugs, fight fever, restrict diet. Going after it with anything else could do more harm than good, so we treat what we can see…" It was getting too hot in there now, the early summer heat beating through the window without mercy, a bead of sweat trickling down Amanda's chest, on its merry way to some unseen destination between her breasts. Realizing that he'd been staring, totally fixated, and hoping no one had noticed, he glanced away. "Until we diagnose what we can't see."

"Could the contaminant be in the drinking water?" Ben asked. "I know that's the obvious question, and you've probably already considered it. But I have to ask."

"I don't think it's what anybody's drinking, because everybody would be sick, or at least a lot more people would be if they were drinking the contaminant. Something I'd like to do anyway, to be on the safe side, is filter the hospital's drinking-water supply, because that's where you always have to look first."

"What if we boil the water before we consume it?" Ben asked. "Will that get rid of the contaminant?"

"It can in most cases. But I still want it filtered as well, to be on the safe side."

"Leaving us in another dilemma, trying to figure out how to get a filter system." Ben sighed heavily. "These weren't the things they told us about in medical school."

"Med school teaches us to be doctors, real life teaches us to be doctors who know how to function in the world," Jack said, then shut his eyes and totally zoned out. Mentally stepped away from the office for a moment.

"I'll bet Jack's coming up with another idea," Amanda whispered, observing him, totally caught up by his process.

He didn't respond for another minute as both Amanda and Ben stayed dead silent, observing him. Measuring their breaths. Then he opened his eyes, nodded, didn't smile, but his frown disappeared and Amanda and Ben finally breathed normally again.

"It's only a temporary fix, because at some point, when we isolate the bug we're dealing with, we're going to have to take care of it with more than a patch. But for now we could make a filter. Or filters. I've done this before and I'm betting we'll find everything we need in the village. Maybe put Ezequiel in charge of going down there and scavenging the parts. Then put his resourcefulness to use by letting him recruit volunteers to help in the assembly.

"Keep in mind this isn't a cure. Not even close. But we'll filter the water then boil it, and that goes for what we consume as well as what's used for sponge baths and washing our hands."

He finally managed to wedge himself between Amanda and Ben then opened the door, glad to make his imminent escape. "I'll make the supply list and give it to Ezequiel and hope we can get this project started later today."

"Then while he's out hunting for the supplies, would you like to make a house call with me?"

Amanda asked, stepping in front of him, blocking his way out.

"House call?"

She nodded. "It's a dicey drive to one of the outlying villages. Nice people, fairly isolated. Don't really want to do it alone. Normally I take Ezequiel, but as he's going to be busy…"

He saw the corners of her mouth turn up, saw mischief start to twinkle in her eyes. "Something tells me you don't want me for my abilities as a doctor." He purposely avoided looking at the damp area spreading even more across the front of her T-shirt. Something about Amanda glistening with sweat was more provocative than he cared to deal with.

"And on my sister's less-than-clever attempt to manipulate, I take my exit," Ben said, sliding between them and on out into the hall.

"Okay, so maybe I do have an ulterior motive. The vehicle I'm going to use is a little touchy," she said, her grin widening. "Sometimes it needs help."

"As in?"

"A push start."

"Oh. You mean you push, I steer?"

"However you like it, Dr. Kenner," she said, sweeping out of the room. "I'll be ready to roll, *or push,* in thirty minutes. Wear your hiking boots, by the way. Half the journey's by foot."

A trek through the jungle with Amanda... He didn't know which would be more threatening— the pumas, skunks and wild boars they might encounter, or Amanda. Somehow, he thought Amanda. "This just keeps getting better and better. Next you'll be telling me we're going to have to ford a river."

She smiled. "Just a small river. You won't have to carry me, if that's what's worrying you. Currents aren't strong, water's not deep."

Actually, carrying her sounded like the high point. "Depends on whose currents you're talking about. And the water's always deep, Amanda. Sometimes you don't know it until you're in it." Or drowning.

One final sweep through the isolation ward to check on the kids, and he was on his way out the door. Truthfully, he didn't mind going to treat some villagers, but his preference would have been staying here, with the proper supplies, to do the job he was supposed to be doing. It was frustrating, being so…impotent. This HAI should have been diagnosed and treatment for it well under way.

What frustrated him even more than the fact that he hadn't even begun was what he knew he'd find when he did get started. It was going to be a simple bacterium. Easy to diagnose under normal circumstances, easy to treat. Except here it was turning into a convoluted mess because there was nothing he could do about it…*yet*. No control of what he should have been able to control…a situation that wasn't making him clamor to stay in medicine. At least, not right now.

Seeing Ezequiel running up the path toward him, though, made him wonder what he did clamor for. Was there anything any more?

"Now's a good time to come see my lights, Doc K," Ezequiel said, almost breathlessly. Jack rubbed his forehead, hoping it would quell his rising frustration. Then braced himself not to show it to Ezequiel. "Now's a *great* time to see your lights!" he said with more enthusiasm than he expected, then allowed Ezequiel to lead him down the corridor and around a couple of corners, until they reached the small room where the boy put on a grand ceremony of opening the door with a swoosh.

"Ta-dah," Ezequiel sang, stepping back so Jack could see every last one of them. "Isn't it beautiful?"

"It's beautiful." Jack was so touched by the sentiment, a hard lump formed in his throat, and he fought to swallow it back. A water bottle, a few lights…things no one ever thought about, yet they meant so much to Ezequiel. "What I want you to do now is to plan how we're going to string up the lights in the public areas."

"I don't know…" Ezequiel began shaking his head "…what they are."

"The waiting room, the place where the receptionist sits. The porch outside. I think Doc Ben's office would be good, too." He watched the boy's eyes grow wide from excitement. "Can you draw pictures, Ezequiel?"

"A little."

"Then here's what we need to do. I want you to draw a picture of each room, then draw in where you'd like to hang the lights." It was a little bit of a stall, but one, along with the water-filter assignment, that would keep Ezequiel busy until he returned from the house call. "We'll use those drawings to show us where to hang the lights."

"Tonight? Can I hang the lights tonight? And you'll help me, *please?*"

How could he refuse an invitation like that? Ezequiel was about as captivating a kid as he'd ever known. Shame the boy didn't have a real home. Damn shame he couldn't take him in, take him back to Texas since no one would even care, give him a real home and… No! This was what had cost him Rosa. That kind of thinking. The first thought that seemed so easy, so right. But doing the right thing, the easiest thing had turned so wrong. Wrong for her. Wrong for Ezequiel.

Besides, the boy was cared for. Being educated.

Fed. Clothed. He was lucky. *Leave it alone,* Jack cautioned himself. Leave it the hell alone, or it would break his heart the way Rosa had. "Sure. After dinner. Don't know if we can get it all done, but we can give it a good start.

"But before you do that, I have something else for you to do. Something very important that will help keep people in the hospital from getting sicker. It's a big job, Ezequiel," he cautioned as he grabbed the boy's undivided attention. "And you're the only one I can count on to do it for me."

Jack spent the next few minutes explaining what they were going to do with the filters, then he gave Ezequiel a list of commonplace supplies he needed from the town. Between that and the stringing of the lights, Ezequiel had some busy hours ahead of him. Hours, Jack hoped, that would be valuable to a boy who had so little in the world.

"He really idolizes you," Amanda said, once Ezequiel had scampered off to the village in search of filter materials. "Then after you gave him all that authority…you may have a friend for life, if you want it."

"I don't get involved," Jack said, turning on his gruff self.

"That's not what I'm seeing. Every time you look at Ezequiel, I see…something even bigger than involvement."

"Then you're not seeing right. Kids are okay as patients, but that's as far as I ever get involved with them. They're…needy. I don't need needy."

Amanda actually laughed. "That's supposed to convince who? You or me? Because I see need, Jack, every time Ezequiel comes around. And it's not his need I'm seeing."

"Then get glasses."

Jack started to march off, but Amanda ran to catch up with him. "Why is it so difficult admitting that you care for Ezequiel?"

"It's not. I like him. End of story." No way in hell he was one of those people who wore his heart on his sleeve. He'd loved a child once, she'd died. He couldn't go through it again. More than that, he wouldn't go through it again. And Amanda wasn't going to goad that story out of him because she'd get all sympathetic, try saying the right things, try being supportive, try making the situation better. But he wasn't the kind of person who required that. Being left alone was all he needed.

"If you say so, but—"

"But nothing. Let's go get that car push started and get out of here. Okay? Otherwise I'm sure I can find a few patients in the clinic who'd like me to see them."

"You're not really such a hard case, Jack," she said as they headed across the road, Jack trying his utmost to stay ahead of her and Amanda trying her utmost to keep up with him. "And I'm not fooled. But if you want me to pretend I believe you, I will." She added under her breath, "Even if I don't."

"You never let anyone get in the last word, do you?"

Pushing the door, she held it open for Jack then as he passed by her said, "Not if I can help it."

Glancing in the rear-view mirror, they were already off the hospital compound and Jack was still pushing the rusty bucket of bolts formerly known as a car. It was a tiny thing, two seats, no glass in the side windows, very loud once it got going, and right now it wasn't going. But watching him put his muscle into the effort was funny. Jack Kenner was all kinds of interesting, and the more she was around him, the more she admired.

Of all the times to meet someone like him, it had to be now. Sure, he wasn't responsive in the way most women wanted a man to be responsive. But she wasn't most women, and here, in Argentina, she *had* seen him watching her in off moments. The Amanda he was watching, though, wasn't really her. At least, not in the true sense, because in another two weeks, when she returned to Texas, she'd be back to her usual persona.

She was flattered, though, whichever Amanda she was. More than that, she liked the tingle she got when he was watching. No denying it was sexual.

But some of it was about knowing what her two different sides were about now. Jack had done that for her. Given her a part of herself no one in her life had even wanted to talk about, which better allowed her to understand why Argentina welcomed her, why she thrilled to that wildness it ignited in her, a wildness that didn't want to be tamped down. And why Texas tamped all that down in her, sent her back to the woman her parents had raised her to be…proper and reserved. She felt Argentina, she dwelled in Texas. Not quite polar opposites, she supposed, but definitely a night-and-day situation. Only which was night in her, and which was day?

Glancing back in the mirror again, she decided she liked being whichever one got to see Jack reasoning with an old car. Telling it to please start. No anger, no shouting, no grumpiness. Just gentle persuasion aimed at something that should have been relegated to the scrap heap a decade ago. "Maybe if you could push it just a little bit faster…" she yelled to him, then spun to watch his reaction in the rear-view mirror.

His reaction was fast, and totally unexpected. He sprinted from the back of the car to the driver's side, which had no door, and pointed to the ground.

"What?" she asked, amused.

"Get out."

"And do what?"

"We'll get another ride."

"This ride is perfectly fine. It always starts."

"And wastes time. So get out or I'll…"

"What? What will you do, Jack?" He wasn't scowling now, wasn't smiling, either. More like… simmering, ready to ignite. But ignite how? *How?* That was always the question with Jack. And she never knew the answer. Didn't matter, though, because it stirred her up, thinking about all the possibilities. Jack good, Jack bad. All the same. All so sexy.

"I'm going to ford that stream," he said, then bent down and scooped her into his arms.

Next thing she knew, she was staring him straight in his gorgeous dark brown eyes. Giddy to be there, taken aback that she actually was because she and Jack were so close Amanda could practically feel the prickle of his rough stubble on her cheek. Causing definite heart palpitations, maybe some vertigo. "Make sure we don't drown," she finally managed, when she'd recovered her wits. Somehow she had the feeling she was already part way there.

As it turned out, Jack carried her to the end of the street, to the village's only taxi. A pleasant ride in his arms, all things considered. Then they got into the taxi, which would take them to the end of the next road, and from there they'd walk.

"Were you trying to impress me with your brute strength, Dr. Kenner?" she asked, fully expecting his usual sarcastic remark as she crawled into the backseat. Instead, he said nothing for what seemed like an eternity. His usual behavior and she was getting used to it—him staring at her. This time, though, he was staring so intently she felt a warm blush creeping to her cheeks.

Then, finally. "*Were* you impressed?"

She wanted to find an appropriate comeback. Wanted to say something sassy and provocative and pithy. But sitting there together on the seat, their shoulders touching, and their thighs, she didn't want to be touching because the more she thought about it the harder her heart pounded, and the harder her heart pounded the more she was afraid he would hear. Or she'd actually go woozy from the blood rushing from her brain to her heart. Or worst of all, in this moment of panic and panic attack and uncertainty, she'd open her mouth and say something totally, utterly stupid. So she simply nodded. Then looked out the window for the rest of the ride to the end of the road, wondering with every revolution of the tire what was coming over her.

The rest of the ride couldn't have come soon enough, because by the time the taxi let them out at virtually nowhere, she so wanted to get away from Jack that Amanda practically ran to the trail head.

"What's going on?" Jack asked, turning to watch the taxi drive away.

"Everything. The hospital's situation, trying to find out who I am. I'm not sure I know what I'm doing anymore."

"You're doing what you have to do," he said, picking up both their backpacks as they headed off toward the path leading to their house call. "Dealing with what you have to deal with."

"You don't think it's the right thing, do you? Trying to find out—"

"I don't think it's any of my business," he interrupted.

"You made it your business when you told me you thought I might be Mapuche."

"Your choice, Amanda. Not mine." He held out his hand to help her over a log on the path. "For what it's worth, would it do any good if I told you I think your search is going to be more frustrating than productive, that you're looking for the proverbial needle in the haystack? And that I know you're *going* to go through with it no matter what anyone says? Which I admire."

"Probably not," she said, enjoying the feel of his hand. Rough, used to hard physical work. Not like most doctors with their velvety skin. "Or maybe a little."

He sighed heavily, still holding her hand as they continued down the trail. "Let me get through the crisis at the hospital, then I'll make a call or two and see what I can find. But I'm not promising anything. Understand that, I'm not going to promise you anything."

"You already did," she said, afraid to even wiggle her fingers lest he remember he had her hand and let go. "They lied to me, Jack. I don't know why they did, but I do know my parents lied to me." She'd never said that aloud before, but to reveal such a dark secret to Jack was easy. He made it easy. "By not lying to me, you're giving me the biggest promise I've ever had."

"Have you talked to Ben about any of this?" He actually gripped her hand a little harder, started to squeeze.

She shook her head, forced to pull her hand from his when his grip started to become painful. Wondering why he'd gone from tender to tense. Probably because he truly didn't want to be involved, she decided. None of this had been in the bargain when he'd agreed to come to Argentina, and she'd so handily dragged him into it. Something she was beginning to regret but didn't know what to do with.

"It would hurt him, and I won't do that. My brother's had his own share of problems over the years, and I won't add to them. The thing is, I just want to know. It won't make any difference in who I am, or what I do, but…"

"But you have the right to know who you are. I supposed we all do, don't we?"

"Then even though you don't agree with what I'm doing, you understand."

"I understand. And you're right, I don't agree, but if I were in the same place, I'd probably be doing the same things you are, the same things you did in the past. So, couldn't you simply ask your parents?"

She wanted him to take her hand again, stepped up next to him in case he wanted it, too. But the offer wasn't there. In fact, Jack took the lead, went a few steps ahead of her. Seemingly protective, but was he really just trying to keep his distance?

"I never told them I was looking for my records, but my dad found out. Then my mother was diagnosed with cancer, and he begged me to stop. Said it would kill her if she ever found out. So I stopped. Called off my lawyer. Mother survived the cancer, but now…she's frail."

"Your dad?"

"Died," she said. "Begging me, on his death bed, not to continue looking. The thing is, Jack, my parents weren't monsters who bullied me or ever treated me badly. I was cherished, they gave me everything. So while I want to do this, and I need to do this…"

"You're conflicted."

"Like you can't even begin to imagine. And maybe starting the search again is selfish of me, because it really *won't* make a difference in my life."

He stopped, and turned to face her. "Except there's this hole in your soul that needs to be filled. It's awful not feeling complete, and I'm sorry you have to go through it."

She looked up at him, a stray tear sliding down her cheek. Sniffed. Then nodded. "I wasn't sure anybody could sympathize. You know, great life, every advantage, what difference does anything else make?"

"It makes a difference." Stepping forward, he stopped and brushed away a tear with his thumb. "I don't know how I can help you, but if you give me a few days, until I can get the HAI isolated and figure out a way to prevent it, I'll make those calls. See if I can get back in touch with an old friend who runs an orphanage down there. He may be a good resource for you."

"Thank you," she said, her voice subdued. "That means more than you can know."

Impulsively, she stood on tiptoe to brush a kiss on his cheek, but as she pressed herself closer to Jack, it was far closer than any friendly thank-you kiss would ever call for, and their proximity, mixed with the blistering noontime heat... It was smothering him, betraying him in ways he'd never experienced before. The melting of will, the melting of soul... The physical throb of need arising so quickly and intensely there was nothing he could do to stop it.

Just this once he wanted to give in to it. Not tamp it down or deny it, but satisfy the curiosity, the hunger. It was all he would, or could, allow.

But his heart…it was beating so heavily against her chest she would feel it. Would she know that she did crazy things to him he wanted to control? But couldn't? Would she hear the crazy thoughts in his head? The confusion? The argument?

It was either time to step up or step back. And nothing in him was going to let him step back.

One quick kiss to his cheek, her usual, but it was different. And the way he was staring at her… could he see it? See the feelings she'd fought in the taxi ride, that urgency to have more of him when he clearly didn't want the same thing? Or else why this hesitation? Why the stare? Maybe he felt it, too? That rising heat? That convulsive urge? Felt it, didn't know what to do with it, didn't want to get sucked in? Yet he wasn't backing away.

Amanda instantly felt self-conscious about this untempered emotion about to erupt in her, but not enough that she could, or would, look away from him once their eyes met. And fixed. The total awareness passing between them in that mo- ment… For the first time in her life she understood the difference between what she needed and what she wanted.

And it didn't have the dizzying effect she might have expected. Rather, it inspired in her more appreciation for this man—his looks, the lingering trace of aftershave, the tender way he took another step forward, and rather than crushing her with urgency slid his hand around her waist, to the small of her back, and simply caressed her in this moment of uncertainty. With so much patience. And, oh, he had the patience of a saint.

"This is dangerous," she whispered, tilting her face to his until her lips were so close to his she could almost feel the quiver of his flesh on her.

"You're dangerous," he whispered back, his caress hardening as he pulled her against him.

Her lips curved into a sensual smile. "Want to see how much?"

"Here? In the open?" He arched wicked, wicked eyebrows over those dark eyes of his. Eyes that promised to burn right through her.

Amanda drew in a breath, felt it shudder all the way down to her lungs, then pulled him just that fraction of an inch closer, that tiny little measure that made all the difference between possibility and reality, then covered his mouth with hers in a hungry kiss.

Jack responded instantly, returning a kiss much more demanding than her own. And his mouth… so warm. The caress of his lips much softer, yet harder than she could have ever imagined, as he tasted with his tongue, and she opened her mouth with a low moan to welcome all he was offering.

There was nothing tentative in this first kiss. Nothing to explore, nothing to discover for the first time because the need was too great, too fast. The kiss was so new yet so familiar.

Then, as Amanda curled her fingers around Jack's neck, pulling him even closer, Jack pressed his erection into her pelvis, and suddenly the place, the time were gone to them as the ancient cadence doubled its tempo, infusing them with its beat.

Never before had she snaked her leg up a man's leg, yet as her left leg found its way along his, moving ever so slow upward over his thigh, there was no hesitancy in going where this was leading. No thoughts, only responses.

But when he slid his hand underneath her ascending leg, and caressed the back of it, she gasped with pleasure, allowing her pelvis to join in the primal sway with his. Slow, sensual movement. She was caught in the feel, a pure, raw savoring. Couldn't stop. Didn't want to stop. Swaying… pounding…

The feel of his hand slipping under her shirt, pushing aside her bra, finding her breast…

She moaned at the sensation, ready to start the fumble of zippers and buttons and all the things that stood in the way, but when the second moan escaped her, she felt him stiffen. Felt him pull his hand back, slip it away from her.

"What?' she whispered, opening her eyes to see…regret. Then feel her own regret start to slide down over her. "Jack, we…"

He nodded as he let her leg slip back down his. "I know," he said, his voice hoarse. "Duty calls."

"Duty calls," she repeated, tugging her clothes back into place, trying to tug her heart back into place. But it was the stubborn one. The one refusing to budge. So it was up to her to step away, which was what she did. Stepped away from Jack, bent to pick up her backpack, then sighed the biggest sigh of regret in her life. "So…"

Grabbing his own backpack, he nodded. "So…"

And that was all they said for the next few moments as they both turned longing glances at the Pampas grass, and what that particular patch of grass might have turned into. A memory. *Almost* a memory.

CHAPTER SIX

As THE crow would fly, the hike to *Santo Maria del Rastro* was just at a mile. On that hike, with every last step of it he took, he alternately kicked himself for what had almost happened, and what hadn't happened. Of course he'd wanted that kiss. Wanted more. Had known he shouldn't, but hadn't been able to stop himself, no matter what he'd known. Sure, Amanda had been playing with flirtation almost from the moment he'd arrived, and he'd been enjoying it. All of it. That was all it should have been, though, and all it would have been if he'd had a clear thought in his head. Or an ounce of will.

But the woman was driving him insane in ways he hadn't known he could be driven, and there was only so much resistance in him.

He wasn't whole, though, and she deserved

someone who wasn't broken, the way he was. Needed someone stronger to help her through what might be coming. Right now he might be the best available, but in the long-term...

Long-term? Hell, what was that? He didn't have a long-term, which was ultimately what had smacked him into the realization that he had to keep his distance now, even though they had amazing chemistry. She needed more than that chemistry to get her through. He knew that, she didn't. Not yet. But in time...

Damn, this wasn't working out the way it should.

"So, I'll be seeing the women and children in the church," Amanda said, breaking into his thoughts. She was pointing to the bare white wooden structure standing prominently in the middle of the road, the village focal point with everything else growing up around it—the houses, the handful of shops, the school. "Men are going to see you..."

She spun around, smiled mischievously, and nodded in the direction of an old gas station. Dilapidated, with thirty-year-old outdated pumps, and weeds half as high as the windows, not to mention an old hound dog napping lazily in the dirt outside the front door, it hadn't seen much attention for a while. But, then, neither had the proprietor napping alongside his dog, not in the dirt but in a rusty old yard chair that had passed its prime a decade previously.

To refocus his thoughts, pull him back into the moment, Jack blinked hard. "I thought we were making a house call, as in one stop."

"We are. One stop for you, one stop for me. That's the way it usually turns out. They hear a doctor is coming to the village, and aches and pains pop up. Oh, and expect payment for your services. People here want to pay for what they get, usually not in money, but we do take fruits, vegetables, handcrafts… We can use the food, and sell the rest and use the funds for the hospital. But we don't take animals, because we don't kill animals for food, and we can't afford pets, unless someone gives you laying hens or a goat, in which case I'll send Hector up with the Jeep tomorrow to get them. The hospital can always use fresh eggs and milk."

"You can get here by Jeep?" Jack asked.

"From the other end of town. It's a long, winding road in, takes forever, but it's accessible."

"Then why did we walk?" The Jeep would have made things so much less complicated.

"Because walking is faster and the overall distance is shorter. And I love the scenery coming in from that direction. It's good exercise, too, and I like to walk. Don't get the chance too often."

"If I'd taken the lead, would I have gotten to examine my patients in the church while you saw yours in the old garage? Or do I pretty much not get choices in any of this?"

Amanda forced a laugh, one that sounded like she was still under the effect of the Pampas grass. "Oh, I think you took the lead."

Of course he had. He'd wanted to. But she'd been a willing participant. Something he wasn't about to point out for fear of where it would go. "Let's just get on with what we came here to do, okay? I've got to get back to Caridad, and standing here talking isn't getting anything done." He really wasn't so grumpy as he and Amanda parted ways in the middle of the road. Frustrated, maybe. And disoriented, because even with all the cautions and warnings he'd been mulling over since that almost-moment, he still wanted to kiss her. Didn't matter where it would go, or not go, he still wanted to kiss her.

"Okay," he called, struggling to sideline his rising frustration and focus on the work, as he signaled for the few men standing around to follow him, instructing them to step around the hound dog. Which didn't matter, as the dog only barely opened an eye, saw no threat to his domain, and went right back to snoring. Pretty much the same thing his owner did, too. In an unsettling way, he wondered if that was his life in the future…life without medicine if that was what he decided. Or without Amanda.

Well into the third hour, and too busy to think about Amanda, Jack had patients everywhere. On stools, sitting on the floor. A couple of them were tinkering with auto parts and watching a rerun of an old American movie, translated into Spanish, in black and white. Two of them were engaged in a game of checkers, while another one was actually huddled over a workbench, repairing a small motor. Amazingly, the garage was clean. Not spotless, but good enough to serve its function as a makeshift exam room. He'd found an old chrome-plated table, pushed it to the back, and discovered it sturdy enough to suffice for the cursory exams he was performing.

So far he'd seen nothing startling, nothing even noteworthy. Some arthritis, a sinus infection, indigestion, a wart. Then Alfonse Macias appeared, and that's when Jack's uneventful day turned itself completely around.

"Where does it hurt?" Jack asked the gray-haired man, recognizing excruciating pain the instant he saw it. Alfonse was ghost-white, his eyes hollow and vacant. His hands trembled. Every few seconds he flinched in paroxysms of pain. *"Dónde duele?"* Jack tried again in his best, fractured Spanish, kicking himself for not learning more of the language when he'd lived here before.

"Aquí mismo. En mi vientre." Alfonso pointed to his lower belly and Jack got the meaning.

Rather than poking the exact spot Alfonso was indicating, Jack probed off to the right, the lower abdominal quadrant, to be specific, and he was pretty sure what the response to that would be. Alfonso groaned then doubled over, giving Jack his answer. *"El dolor. Cande tempo?"* How long have you been in pain? Simple question, and he wished to God Ezequiel was here to do the translating, because Alfonso answered him but too fast, and Jack didn't catch a word of it. So he turned to the three or four men still waiting to be seen and asked, "Did anyone understand what he just said?"

An older man, one fully invested in watching the TV, didn't bother turning around when he answered, "He was sick to his stomach for two days, then the pain started, and he's had that for three days."

Yet he was still up and walking around. Apparently, Alfonse Macias was a man with strong stamina, because most people would have dropped dead from some kind of infection by now. Acute appendicitis would do that, except, apparently, not to Alfonso. At least, not yet.

"What are our options?" Jack asked Amanda, minutes later.

"Do you think he's perforated?" she asked, rushing behind him across the road, on the way back to the gas station.

"It's hard to tell. He's in a lot of pain, but the man's been sick for a little while, so there's no way of knowing if he's perforated, has some kind of periappendiceal abscess, or even diffuse peritonitis. He told me he wants pills so he can feel better when he goes to work later on today. I told him he couldn't work, he told me I couldn't stop him. I told him that I wouldn't have to stop him, that his appendicitis would. And let's just say an argument ensued."

"Who won?"

"He will, if we save his life. And that's assuming he's still at the gas station and hasn't gone on to work or some other place a man in his condition doesn't need to be going."

"Well, we can give him pills, but not until after

we get him to the hospital and get his appendix out. He'll just have to know it's not negotiable."

Easier said than done. Jack knew that, so did Amanda. But she was an incurable optimist, and he liked watching that in her. Liked her sense of purpose. In this case, though, no matter how much optimism she had, or how large her sense of purpose, the longer the delay between diagnosis and surgery, the more likely there would be serious complications arising. Good stamina or not, Alfonso had a rough road ahead of him, and Jack even doubted the man would consent to go to the hospital, let alone stay there for the few days that would be required.

"So, while it may not be negotiable, tell me how we're going to get him to the hospital, because he's refusing to budge for me. Which makes me wonder, is there anything we can do here?"

Amanda stopped just short of the door, looked down at the old hound dog, which hadn't budged an inch in the past hour, then she looked at Jack. "We can't do an emergency appendectomy here, if that's what you're thinking. Wilderness-type procedures are fine if there aren't other options, but we have other options."

He shrugged. "I'm just saying…"

"I know what you're saying, and I know you're used to working miracles in places no one else could, but, Jack…" She stepped around him and went inside first, only to find Alfonse Macias sitting straight up in an old wooden chair, out to the world. Totally unconscious.

"When did this happen?" Jack asked the man who was sitting next to Alfonso, leaning his shoulder into him to keep him upright.

"Right after you left," the man said. "Shut his eyes, fell over on me."

"I guess this solves our first problem." Amanda was already on her knees next to Alfonso, taking his vital signs. "Jack," she said, discovering only a faint, thready pulse.

He didn't even have to look at her to recognize the tone in the way she spoke his name. They were in serious trouble. "How long will it take to get transport?"

"We don't have transport, except the Jeep, and

at its fastest..." She sucked in a sharp breath as she wrapped the blood-pressure cuff around Alfonso's arm. "If we're lucky, from the time we call to get Hector started on his way here until we have Alfonso on the operating table, two and a half hours. Maybe three."

Jack groaned. "So, I'll make the call," he said, pulling out his cell phone then going outside, hoping for clear reception. Which, of course, he did not get. No signal, not a crackle, not a buzz. Nothing. Damn it to hell, that man was going to die and there was nothing they could do. They couldn't operate here, they had no equipment, not to mention the huge fear of the infection they'd find once they opened him up. No matter which way this went, Alfonso was a ticking time bomb. Yet how could they get him to the hospital?

He was the problem-solver, wasn't he? The one called out to places all around the world to fix something. Relatively speaking, this was a simple problem. Getting his patient from point A to point B. Simple...

Sighing, Jack shut his eyes a moment and

cleared his mind. Then he opened his eyes to an entirely new focus, turned round, looked at the various people wandering up and down the road. Assessed his options and came to the immediate conclusion there was only one thing to do. He needed a truck. Right now! "A truck!" He shouted at the top of his lungs. *"Necesito un camión. Por favor, alguien. Necesito un camión."*

Several people looked at him, one old man even started to approach, then changed his mind and turned off in another direction. Of course, why would anybody respond? They didn't know him. Had never seen him before. And here he was, some lunatic standing in the middle of the street shouting for a truck. But without a way to get Alfonse Macias out of here, he would die. Even with a way to evacuate him, his chances weren't good. A truck, a car...anything. *"Necesito un—"* He started to call out again, but was interrupted by a tap on his shoulder. The old man who'd almost approached him was standing there, holding out a set of keys.

"Behind my house," he said in broken English.

Then pointed to a white, wood-frame house half a block away. "My truck."

"Gracias. Gracias tanto," Jack said, grabbing the keys and running toward the truck as fast as he'd run in a good long time.

Last time he'd run this hard and fast he'd been looking for Rosa. They'd taken her, he'd been trying to find her, frantically running from house to house, building to building, searching... Blinking hard, he tried shutting out that image, shutting out that day. But it never completely shut out. Even as he engaged the twenty-year-old pickup truck and headed toward the garage, he was still back at that day, at that moment when they'd ripped her from his arms and surrounded him, pinned him to the wall so he couldn't go after them...go after Rosa.

For a moment he wondered about Amanda, almost pictured her being ripped from the arms of someone who loved her. But that image he blanked out as he ran inside the garage, flying by the hound dog so fast the beast actually got up and moved a foot away, then plopped down and returned to its nap. "It's not the best transportation, but we can make it work," he said, watching Amanda, who was still at Alfonso's side, but now prepping his arm to insert an IV.

"He's running a low fever," she said, while she swabbed the skin of his underneath forearm. "And he did respond to me, said he's not in too much pain." She smiled. "A lie, because he still wants that pill so he can go to work later on. So, where'd you get the truck?"

Jack shrugged. "I asked, someone answered."

"Amazing people," she said, taking the IV catheter and nodding toward the bag of normal saline. "Would you hook it up when I get the needle in? I figured you'd find a way to get him to the hospital, so I thought I might as well get the IV in him now, in case…"

She didn't say the rest of the words. Didn't have to. The implications were dire. They were about to haul a critically ill man over a bumpy road for the next hour in the back of an open pickup truck. Getting him to the hospital alive would be the miracle. What they'd have to do to keep him alive, he wasn't even going to guess. "Can somebody here drive us?" Jack asked the group of men that had now grown to well over a dozen.

One intrepid soul stepped forward. He didn't look to be much more than Ezequiel's age. But he held out his hand for the keys and Jack didn't refuse. Instead, he instructed several of the men to carry Alfonso to the truck, to keep him flat, to try and not bounce him around. Surprisingly, when they got there, the back of the truck, which had been stacked with crates, was empty, except for the fifteen or so blankets and pillows that had been spread out. And no one was around. Not one single, solitary person loitered to watch. It was as if they did their good deeds as a matter of course, then went on to the next thing. *The way every society should be,* he thought as he crawled into the bed of the truck next to Alfonso, then offered Amanda a hand to crawl up into the back with him. "I didn't get to see all my patients," he said as the truck rolled slowly down the road, with the boy driver in charge of their journey now. "I think I'd like to come back."

Amanda smiled. "It's addictive, isn't it?"

"What?"

"Practicing medicine this way. Practicing it at this basic level. It's different. Exciting."

"If you like practicing medicine," he said, placing his hand on Alfonso's wrist to take a pulse.

"If you like practicing medicine," Amanda repeated, "which you do, Jack."

He shook his head. "Past life, different man."

"Why?"

"I'm not the same man I was when I graduated from medical school."

"We all change. Hopes, dreams, goals. They always change when we get into the real world and assume our own responsibilities. I'm not the same woman I was when I graduated, and I pray to God I'm better, more compassionate, more observant, not only of a patient's physical condition but of his or her overall condition."

"I'm glad it works for you," he said sincerely.

"But it works for you, too. Just look at what you do."

"I diagnose HAIs, or isolate a virus or bacterium. And I don't even do that anymore, except when I get dragged into it."

"Dragged? I don't think you staying involved has anything to do with getting dragged. I mean, I don't know why the reticence, Jack, but your heart isn't in being reluctant. Because you do get involved. Just look at you right now, riding in the back of this truck, saving this man's life on a bumpy road. How much more involved does it get than this?"

"I'm not some inhumane bastard who'd let someone suffer. But I'm not...you. Not a do-gooder. Not someone who has to be involved on the very basic or personal level of patient care. Not anymore. Been there, done it all, discovered it wasn't for me." Because failure was the deepest, darkest pit of misery he'd ever known. And that failure was the hole in his own soul.

"Look, I know what you're doing. I recognize the lead-up to the pep talk. Rah, rah, stay in medicine. I appreciate your concern, but it isn't going to work because I don't know what I'm going to do after this. Maybe leave, maybe stay, maybe spend the rest of my life in indecision. That's who I am now. I'm impermanent. No commitments to anything other than the job I'm doing at the moment. And, sure, I can help you at Caridad, and I probably will from time to time when I can.

"But I'm not you or Ben or any of the other doctors who can do this in the way you all do because I just…I just can't get that committed. To anything. So if that makes me a bastard, then I am. But I'm not going to hang around and pretend I'm something I'm not just because you and I might…"

"Might what, Jack?" she asked.

"Might, at some point in time, get something going. It's out there, Amanda. You and me. We're both adults, we see what's going on between us. The flirtation, the looks. The kiss. It wouldn't take much to tip us over to the next level, and I'm a man who could be tipped. I'll admit it. You're driving me crazy in that regard. But anything we do, anything we have…" He shook his head. "Just don't go getting any ideas that this will lead to a happily ever after, where we both stay here together and help your brother with Caridad. Like I said, I don't do that."

"Well, aren't you just about the most pompous piece of...?"

Alfonso Macais took that moment to stir. In fact, he bolted straight up and tried to rip the IV from his arm. But Jack got hold of him, and helped him back down to a flat position. Then took his blood pressure, listened to his chest, took his pulse, while Amanda readjusted the IV then explained to Alfonso where he was going and what they were doing to help him. It took several minutes, but the man finally did settle down again, shut his eyes, and either went to sleep or simply tried blocking it all out, because he didn't stir again, except for the clenching and unclenching of his left hand.

"Pompous piece of what?" Jack asked, several minutes later. He was pretty sure what she would have said, and he deserved it. But this was the way it was, and it was easier to be clear about who he was rather than let something happen that would hurt her. She was flirting now, having fun with it, no true feelings involved, and that was how it had to stay. Because he cared for Amanda. Truly, deeply cared, and if there was anything in him that would let him get involved more than he already was, it would be his feelings for her.

But in his life he'd loved twice, and watched them die because he hadn't been enough to take care of them. He couldn't do that again. Wouldn't let himself get anywhere near it, especially not with Amanda because she deserved happiness when all he had to offer was grief and letdown.

"Do I really have to answer that?" she said, settling back in at their patient's side. "Because I'd think you already know the answer."

He smiled, but sadly, thinking about his own life without the things he wanted. But at least he knew his limitations. Maybe that was some kind of starting point, if he ever got around to starting again. "I suppose I do, and I deserve it."

"And it's okay with you that people think that?"

"Do I seem like the kind of man who cares what people think?"

"You seem like the kind of man who goes out of his way to fool himself."

"And everybody's entitled to his, *or her,* opinion."

"You were seeing patients in a garage, Jack. That's above and beyond the call. So, yes, I do have my opinion, and I'm entitled to it." She folded her arms across her chest and looked him straight in the eye. "Because I'm right."

Jack's response was to try his cell phone, only to discover he still couldn't get a signal. Well, so much for trying to deflect the moment. Amanda was one persistent woman. And pretty sure of herself. He liked it, actually. Was surprised to find how much he did, as all the women in his past had been…manageable. Submissive. Easy to let come and go without a bother. Amanda was none of those. No one could manage her, and she sure as hell wasn't submissive about anything. But she was worth the bother, and that was what worried him more than he wanted to admit. "So, will the hospital be set up for an appendectomy?" he asked. "I know it can handle simple surgery, but Alfonso isn't going to be a simple case once we get him opened up."

"Can you manage his infection?" Amanda asked.

"Me?"

"You're the infection specialist, and if ever there was a patient at risk for getting some sort of HAI..." She shrugged. "Getting his appendix out will be the simple part."

Rather than answering, Jack simply sighed. One way or another, she was going to keep dragging him in as long as he was here. Only thing was, as long as it was Amanda doing the dragging, he was a willing participant. Too willing, damn it. Way too willing!

"He's stable," Ben said, pulling down his surgical mask. "Pretty sick, but it could have been worse. His appendix was perforated, a fair amount of infection spreading, but I think we got it in time. Good job, getting him here when you did." He gave his sister a warm smile then turned his attention to Jack. "Your supplies will be here first thing tomorrow. You'll have to go down to the landing strip to pick them up. In the meantime, Ezequiel's recruited quite a few people to help you assemble those filters, so anytime you want to get that started..."

And here he'd thought he might take a couple hours off, kick back, enjoy the warm Argentinian evening. Maybe even contemplate the stars. But he'd been on the move from the moment they'd rolled into the hospital and Alfonso had been whisked away to surgery. He'd done rounds on his patients, discovered two more admitted to the ranks of HAIs. He'd done some white-glove cleaning, not because anything in his wards needed it but because he felt helpless, standing around, waiting, trying to fight back thoughts of Amanda always trying to creep in.

Then he'd gone to his hole-in-the wall lab, hoped to find some kind of results in the few little samples he was trying to grow, only to discover nothing. Which led him to believe he was using contaminated medium dishes or faulty swabs. Whatever the case, in a fit of anger he'd swept everything into the trash, kicked the wall, then gone back to his wards and cleaned some more. "Filters," he mumbled.

"Jack's had a rough day," Amanda piped up. "It happens when someone forces some insights on you that you don't want to see, or understand, or admit exist."

"Sounds too complicated for me," Ben said, backing away from the two of them. "Think maybe I'll go grab a quick shower, see if I can find something to eat then check on a few patients before I turn in for the night."

"And I need to make a call to check on some of my patients back in Texas," Amanda said. "I've got good people looking after them, but I still like to keep up." She brushed by Jack. "Oh, and just so I can get my usual last word in, you *are* the kind of man who cares what people think, Jack. You care what they think, how they feel, and most of all you care about taking care of them. Maybe care too much, which leads to a whole different discussion which I don't want to get into right now. The one person you don't care about, though, is you."

"Says the psychologist," he snapped.

"Wrong again, Jack." She paused, laid her palm flat against his chest then looked up at him. "I'm your friend, like it or not." Then she stepped back. "Have fun with Ezequiel and his battalion of volunteers," she said, then slipped away, leaving Jack standing there feeling numb.

This time he didn't watch her walk away, the way he usually did. He was too tired to deal with it. As much as he braced himself against the desires that still gnawed at him, he simply couldn't brace himself well enough. Something to add to his list for a good berating later on. Jack Kenner, willpower of a starving dog standing before a plate of dogfood. But, oh, was Amanda tasty.

CHAPTER SEVEN

"Giardia," he said. It had been diagnosed now, and the result wasn't unexpected, given the symptoms he'd seen. The medicine to treat it was en route, and his work here was, for the most part, close to being done. Most likely he'd be leaving here in the next day or two. Return to Texas, and… Well, he wasn't sure what came after that. He didn't have a life there. Not anymore. Didn't have a life anywhere else, either, and wasn't sure he wanted to get involved in anything that resembled one for a while because of one kiss, five days ago, and he'd been a mess ever since.

"The filters are in place, our patients are recovering, no new cases, and you know how to handle it until I get back to the States and see what I can do to secure a permanent filtration system— I know a couple of corporations that will always make a donation to a good cause. Then I'll over-see the installation when the time comes. But for now..." he shrugged "...there's no reason for me to stay on."

"I think there is," Amanda said stepping up be-hind him. "New case. Child, aged nine. Post-op two days for a compound fracture, right tibia. She fell out of a tree, had a fair amount of bone ex-posed in the wound. We're lucky that Dr. Clayton is volunteering this week because he's one of the best orthopedic surgeons I know, and his repair to the fracture was beautiful. So now the patient's on antibiotics due to the probability of infection stemming from how dirty the wound was when she came in.

"The water filters went on three days ago, Jack, but she was admitted a day after that, and she first started showing HAI symptoms last night. Which means we've still got something the fil-ters aren't getting."

"Damn," he muttered, pounding his fist on the desk. They were standing in Ben's office again, a tight squeeze he'd come to like when he was squeezed in there with Amanda, and hate otherwise.

This morning, though, Jack took particular care not to stand anywhere close to her. In fact, he'd done a brilliant job of avoiding her for the past one hundred and twenty hours, give or take an occasional glance or word in passing, and it had truly been his intention to make his phone call to Richard Hathaway, as he'd promised her, then vanish. Not the best style, but the least complicated in the middle of a situation that had all the potential in the world of turning hugely complicated.

In the long run, better for Amanda, too. Besides, he hated messy goodbyes and this one, he feared, would be very messy. Or maybe he was simply taking the coward's way out, not facing up to the one thing that could actually stop him from leaving. "So, you're sure the symptoms match?" he asked.

"Not only match, they're bad. She's critical, Jack. Yesterday afternoon she was mildly sick. It looked like it might have been a post-anesthesia reaction. Then the overall downgrade of her condition started a couple hours ago, so I'm going to have to arrange transportation to a hospital with pediatric critical care because of her Giardia symptoms, as well as a wound infection that isn't clearing up." Amanda swallowed hard then lowered her voice. "I think one thing is exacerbating another, and we're not equipped to handle it. She's dying, Jack, and we can't save her here."

Without saying a word, Jack spun around and almost knocked Amanda over in his hurry to get to Pediatrics.

"I'm not sure how long it's going to take to get her out of here," Ben said. He was already riffling through his phone index, looking for the right contact. "I'll do the best I can."

"I know you will," Amanda said. Pure, merciless agony was written all over her face. "It's always so difficult when it's a child, isn't it? I mean, it's not easy when it's anybody, but a child…"

Turning away from Ben, Amanda focused on the window opposite him, her mind too preoccupied to fix her attention on anything outside. "Look, there's something I've wondered about lately, Ben. It's been bothering me, but there's never a good time to ask." She shrugged. "Don't think we're going to have one, so…so I'm just going to ask." Pausing, she drew in a deep breath to steady herself. Then turned to face him. "Why did you choose Argentina?"

"What?"

"Argentina. You could have set up a hospital anywhere in the world, but you chose Argentina, and I don't know why you did that. You never told me, and now that I'm discovering who I am, I'm curious. Did you suddenly wake up one morning and think that this is where you wanted to spend the rest of your life? Or was there another reason you chose this country? *This* country. That's what's been bothering me most. Was it a coincidence, or something else?" Now she'd know, once and for all, if her brother stood with her or against her. No turning back.

"I'd read about it," he said, clearly uncomfortable. "Seemed like as good a place as any for a hospital. There was a need. The government's receptive and even welcoming of medical care. So..." he shrugged "...I guess it fit."

"That's it? You read about Argentina, and something in what you read had so much appeal this is where you ended up? Then all these many years later, lo and behold, I'm transformed from Mediterranean into Argentinian because one person in my life saw fit to tell me the truth?" She shook her head vehemently.

"Until today, Ben, I'd have never believed you would lie to me. But that's what you're doing now, isn't it? Lying? And I don't know if you're doing it to protect our parents or to protect me."

She backed away from him, not sure whether to stay there and fight or simply walk away. This was her brother, and she loved him dearly. Nevertheless, he was wrong. Whatever his reason, he was wrong to hold back the truth from her. "I want the truth, and I'm going to get it, one way or another. With or without you, that's a promise. I'm going to find out, because it's my life and I deserve to know."

Drawing in a deep breath, she backed up against

the wall across from his desk, needed it to hold her up. "I love you, and that's not going to change, but after I've learned the answers to the questions I've always had, I hope that doesn't change our relationship. It could, though. Because you know something I should know, and you're like Dad, who spent his last breath telling me to quit searching. Well, I'm not quitting, and I only pray you're not caught up or hurt in this, because this time I'm not backing down. So, let me ask you one more time. Why Argentina?"

"There was a need," he said, without conviction. In fact, he looked miserable.

Ben knew the answers she wanted and wouldn't tell her. What devastated her most, though, was that when Jack had predicted her broken heart, she hadn't expected it this soon. And not because of Ben. Yet his refusal to tell her the truth broke her heart. Probably the first of many other heartbreaks to come, and for a moment she wondered if she really wanted to go through with this. Maybe Jack was right about everything. Maybe she shouldn't.

But it *was* her right to know, no matter what

Ben said or did. So she braced herself for her next words…words she'd never thought she'd have to say. "Then I'm sorry it has to be this way, Ben," Amanda said. "You, of all people, were the one I trusted. The one I've always believed in. But I can't. Not anymore."

"You don't have to do this, Amanda." He held his place apart from her, emotionally and physically, the weight of the world crushing him. "I can—"

"What, Ben? Tell me more lies and hope one of them takes? Hope that I'm gullible enough or desperate enough to believe you again?" She swiped at angry tears then turned toward the door. "I'll be with my patient. Let me know when you've arranged to get her transferred to another hospital."

Perhaps Ben was caught in the middle. Maybe his loyalties were being torn the way hers were. Bitterly torn, but of his own choosing, and there was nothing she could do except hope that someday she'd understand why he'd done what he'd done and be able to forgive him. Now, though, she felt so…alone.

That was the only thing on her mind as she trudged down the hall to the tiny isolation room where her patient was being examined by Jack, who was so totally oblivious to everything but his patient, he didn't even notice Amanda coming up behind him.

"How's she doing?" Amanda asked, watching the meticulous way he changed the dressing on Renata's incision. "Any better?"

He shook his head gravely. "Why didn't you come get me as soon as all this started?"

"What would you have done differently than I did?" she asked, still defensive from her argument with Ben. "And why do you think I'm not capable of taking care of my patient without your interference? You, Ben…you're both alike. You look at me and you think I'm…I'm… You know what? It doesn't matter what you think. What *either* of you think. I'm a good doctor, and I—"

"Amanda," Jack said, his voice barely above a whisper, "can we talk about this when I'm done here?"

"What's there to talk about?"

"Apparently, a lot more than I was aware of."

"Or nothing at all." Because she was talked out, tired of words. Jack and Ben could say or do what they wanted. So could she. *So could she.* "Look, let me help you with this," she said, snapping on gloves and taking her place at the other side of the bed. She looked down, cringed at what she saw. Then her bottled-up anger turned to concern for the child. "It's…" She mouthed the word *"worse."*

He nodded. "But Renata and I have been having a chat," he said, gesturing for Amanda to take the girl's blood pressure. "Even though she won't open those gorgeous brown eyes and look at me, we've come to an understanding. Haven't we, Renata?"

This was Jack at his best, Amanda thought. Where he shone. The man he was meant to be. "If he didn't promise you ice cream, Renata, I'd make him add that to your understanding." Of course, the child didn't understand a word of English. But she truly believed that many people in comas, the way this little girl was, could hear. A voice could be a lifeline. "Or a *palmerita.*"

"Both, if she opens her eyes right now and looks at me," he said, finishing the last of his bandaging.

"Blood pressure's still the same," she said, once she'd removed the cuff from Renata's arm. "Not getting better, not getting worse. Which is good. She's fighting." Lessons to be learned from a child, she supposed. Renata was waging her valiant fight while Amanda was wavering in hers.

"Look, I know she's your patient, and you've got her on metronidazole, but I'd like to suggest adding quinacrine to that."

"Both?" she asked.

"She's got at least one, if not two underlying conditions going on, and my goal right now is getting one of the problems knocked out of her as fast as we can."

"What do you mean, she may have two conditions?"

"Her leg wound is the first thing that worries me. The infection in it's going to turn out to be *Staphylococcus aureus,* a surgical site infection. Probably something she brought in with her when she broke her leg—something that got into the wound before we got to it. Normally, I'd want to diagnose an infection like that with a positive laboratory culture of a swab from the infected site, which we know isn't going to happen. My other choice, something I like to resort to when there are no viable bacteria to culture, is making the diagnosis on the basis of a blood test demonstrating an immune response to toxins following a compatible illness."

"Which we can't do, either." But, oh, how she loved hearing him talk about it. It was technical and exciting, and while to most people it was probably boring, hearing Jack in his element gave her goose bumps. "So, what's your third choice?"

He smiled. "I make a guess. Given the circumstances, the appearance of the wound, and how the surgical site infection developed, then factor in her age and a whole lot of unscientific variables, I'd say it's staph."

"Because Giardia won't erupt in a skin wound."

"Exactly."

"But you said a second diagnosis."

"I'm guessing she's also diabetic. It causes the

body's defenses to go crazy, and even after a night of aggressive treatment she's not responding. *Staphylococcus aureus* and diabetes have a strange little song and dance they like to do together. They act in tandem to force the body's defense systems to hide their antigens to avoid an immune response. They also gang up to kill infection-fighting cells.

"Because people with diabetes are more prone to certain infections, the underlying condition can help the intruding bacteria survive within the host infection-fighting cells, which helps develop resistance to antibiotics. She's resisting the antibiotics you prescribed, so there's something else going on."

Sexy talk again. Okay, so maybe not traditionally sexy, but she was still having goose bumps, and wondering if her feelings for him were deepening because he was her only port in the storm or the only port she *wanted* in her storm. Being around Jack just made things seem manageable, and it was a feeling she liked. One she hadn't had much experience with. "So what you're saying is that one thing doesn't cause the other but assists it."

"Exactly. And because she's at a higher risk for Type 1 diabetes due to her heritage. Probably has a family history of it. Also, I took her blood sugar." He pulled a monitor from his labcoat pocket. "Over two hundred."

"But she was normal last night when I took it," Amanda said, then let out an exasperated sigh. "And she doesn't sustain the fast." Meaning Renata was one of the rare individuals whose blood sugar elevated rather than dropped when she didn't eat. "Which I totally missed."

"Because you weren't looking for it. It would have manifested itself eventually. And in the meantime, you were treating the obvious—an infection, a fracture. But in my medicine I have to look for something other than the obvious."

"Or, if you're like me, you don't see it even when it's slapping you in the face every day of your life." She drew in a ragged breath, shut her eyes, rubbed her forehead. "I don't even know what's going on anymore. Can't focus…"

"You didn't make a mistake."

"Then why do I feel like everything's a mistake?"

"Probably because you're overwhelmed. People who take on life the way you do go through that from time to time."

"As opposed to people like you who take on people like me and tell them they're okay when they're really not?" She didn't want to be angry, didn't want to be hurt. But she was, at herself. "Look. I should have seen it. But I didn't and now look at her."

"Amanda, meet me in the hall. Okay?"

"Fine," she said, wanting to kick a hole through the wall in the hall to which she was being banished. The truth was, he was right to send her out. She wasn't being objective. Wasn't being the doctor Renata needed. So the hall suited her. So did the wall she leaned against to wait for Jack. And the floor she stared at. And the baseboard she kept kicking with the heel of her shoe. It all suited her and if she didn't get a better grip, it would be the only thing suiting her for some time to come.

"She's going to be fine, Amanda, once she's transferred, all the tests are done and her various conditions are diagnosed and treated." He handed the medical chart to the nurse who walked out of Renata's room with him, then went to lean against the wall next to Amanda. "In the meantime, I ordered—"

"You ordered insulin, and simple penicillin, which works best to treat the S. aureus. And the quinacrine. Jack, I…"

He held up his hand to stop her. "It's what I do. Not a big deal."

"Not a big deal? Tell that to Renata's parents. I have an idea they'll tell you what a really big deal it is. So how dare you *not* know this is where you belong? Because people are going to die without you, Jack. There's going to be another outbreak of something someone can't identify, or another child like Renata, who… How can you not see it? Tell me. How can you not see it?"

She slapped her hands on her legs in frustration, spun, and marched out. Out the door. Out into the courtyard. Didn't stop until she was halfway up the steps to her quarters. Even then the only reason she stopped at all was because Jack caught up to her, grabbed hold of her arm and forcibly held her in place.

"What's this about?" he asked.

She didn't spin to face him. Didn't want him to see her anger, her frustration. Her tears. So she stood her ground, stayed rigid, drew in a bracing breath. "I made a mistake."

"What?" he asked. "What, exactly, was your mistake? Because you treated that little girl the way she was supposed to be treated."

"And missed the fact that she's diabetic."

"Because she wasn't displaying symptoms. And the tests haven't been done yet, Amanda. She could be having some kind of blood-sugar reaction due to the trauma. A one-time incident."

"You know that's not true, Jack. If I'd been thorough…"

He let go of her arm. "You were thorough, Amanda. I read your notes, saw what you were doing with her. You conducted the test you had available, and it's exactly what I would have done. Exactly what I did."

"No, it's not, Jack." She whirled to face him, not caring anymore what he saw on her face. "And quit trying to placate me with things that don't matter. Maybe I didn't mess up, but I—"

"What's this really about?" he interrupted.

She shook her head, afraid to speak for fear she'd burst into tears. "Argentina. That's what this is about. I asked him, Jack. I asked Ben why he chose to practice medicine here, and he wouldn't tell me. More than that, I believe he lied to me." Her voice broke into a whisper. "He knows something and he'd rather lie about it than tell me." Finally, the tears came, not in an outburst but in an intermittent trickle down her face.

Without a word Jack wrapped a supportive arm around Amanda's waist and led her up the remaining steps and into their cottage, where he shut the door behind them. "Talk to me," was all he said as he guided her to her side of the room. But she didn't go to her bed, or even to one of the few chairs that sat at odd angles in various corners of the room. Rather, she guided him to the window and looked out, trying to find a shred of composure.

"You know, I don't believe in coincidences, and I told him so. I also told him this could come between us, but it didn't make a difference. I know he cares, I know he loves me, but... How could he do this to me?" Stepping up behind her, Jack wrapped his arms around her, allowing her to relax into his chest, and she was glad for his support, his strength, even if it was hers only for a moment. "I don't understand."

"Did he say anything at all that would give you a clue about what he's hiding?"

"Just that he came to Argentina because there was a need here. But that's not it, Jack. I know my brother, and he's not good at lying. So Argentina *isn't* a coincidence, and Ben would rather split up our family than tell my why he came *here.* We've been so close, and now all I feel is..."

"Betrayed."

"Yes. I guess because I didn't expect he'd ever do something like this, especially after... Ben had

this accident years ago, and we didn't know if…"
Her voice broke. "He wanted to die. He wasn't
fighting back. So I stayed with him, sat in that
hospital room day and night and fought for him.
Missed a whole semester of school because I refused to leave my brother's side.

"Then fought for him again and again over the
next couple years when he needed someone there
to help him through. And I promised him that no
matter what happened, I would take care of him
and make sure he got better. When nobody else
could get him to eat, I could. When he refused
his medications, I was the only one who could
get him to take them. And it went on like this for
months, Jack.

"It's when I knew I wanted to be a medical doctor. I saw my skills, not only at whatever kind of
simple medicine a child could administer but I
saw the psychological side to it as well, and how
a person's psychological makeup is so important
to their physical health. Which is why I became
both a doctor and a psychologist.

"Anyway, later, when Ben and I were talking

about how bad that time had been for him, he promised me he'd do the same if I ever needed it. I mean, it was one of those stupid promises you make in a moment of gratitude or overwhelming emotion, but I've always counted on it, counted on Ben to come through for me. Except he didn't because he's part of the lie. Part of what my parents kept from me."

"Maybe because he *is* trying to take care of you?" Jack asked.

"Take care of me?" She shook her head. "He's hurting me, and he knows it."

She turned to face him finally, and looked up at him. Tears were still glistening in her eyes. "I may lose everything... Maybe I already have. But I can't quit. You told me part of who I am, and now I have to find out the rest because..." she swiped at the tears sliding down her face, then sniffled "...because I was always different. The dark-skinned girl in a fair-skinned family. The one people whispered about. The one the kids made fun of. And, sure, it really doesn't seem like much of a big deal, but when you're growing up different, and people are always staring or pointing fingers, it hurts. People can be cruel."

"I know," he said, thinking back to Robbie. Sweet boy, and people had pointed fingers and stared. Robbie hadn't seen it so much, but *he* had, and sometimes his rage on behalf of his brother had ripped so hard at him he hadn't known what to do with it. Once he'd slammed his fist through the wall, broken a couple of fingers. "People can be cruel."

"The thing is, I want to vindicate my parents. Right now I have such mixed feelings about them, and I hate it. I loved my dad, love my mom and Ben, and I don't want that to change. But it is and I want to stop it. Want things the way they used to be. Want to think about my dad the way I used to when I was daddy's little girl and he called me his princess. I adored him, Jack, and I want to hang on to that. Which means I have to settle it." She drew in a deep breath, squared her shoulders. "Please, tell me. Am I doing the right thing?"

"If this search is what it takes to settle yourself, you're doing the right thing." He hated saying it because he knew the kind of hurt that would inevitably ensue. But he knew what it was like to not know yourself, to stand alone in a crowd. That was where he'd been standing for most of his life. "Let me tell you about the Mapuche, since that's where it all starts. Theirs isn't a prevalent culture in Argentina, as I'm sure you've already discovered. Mapuche, by the way, means native people, or people of the land."

"People of the land," she said, sniffling. "I like that."

Jack chuckled. "So do I. It fits you, because they're a very practical people. They embrace life, and have this way of just being part of their surroundings in vital yet subtle ways."

"It fits you, too. Maybe not in the way the Mapuche would define it, but you do belong to the land, Jack. To the people you serve, in vital and subtle ways."

"Used to," he corrected.

"Still do." She turned around in his arms, and tilted her face to his. "You still do, and I want to help you find that again."

"For me, there's nothing to find." He lowered his head, came within a breath of her lips, and stopped. "But for you, as soon as I figure out why we have a new case of giardiasis here, we'll go south."

"You'll take me?"

"Yes, I'll take you." Take her to his own personal hell so she wouldn't have to face hers alone.

The kiss that came after that was sweet. Tender. Familiar and comfortable. And before he got to the point of arousal or pure, raw desire, he slid out of it. Not because he didn't want more but because he'd just made a promise that scared him. Helping her was one thing. He'd created the monster she would surely discover, and it was his duty to protect her from it. But his feelings were changing. Softening. And that was where the scare factor came in and walloped him in a big way.

"Look, there's this area in the Pampas," he started, hoping his voice didn't sound as uncertain as he was feeling. "It's south and west of Buenos Aires. It's where that orphanage is I mentioned, and the records there go back at least for thirty years. So since your search is going to be like looking for the proverbial needle in a haystack, that's as good a haystack as any to start with."

"Jack," Amanda cried, as a new gush of tears started. "I...I don't know what to say except thank you! I've never had any support in this, and now you... You're doing so much."

"I won't stay, Amanda. Maybe a little while, but this isn't the start of any kind of change of heart for me. I'll help you get situated, make sure you have everything you need, but then I'll be leaving. You've got to understand that. I will not stay."

"I didn't think you would," she said, almost sadly. "But I'm so grateful, Jack. You can't even begin to know what this means to me."

Her gratitude, combined with his confusion and awakenings, then a kiss as passionate as anything anyone had ever laid on him, and in the blink of an eye nothing else mattered. Her arms were around his neck, and he wanted them there. In the second blink, her lips were pressed to his and tongues were already probing, as if this was customary foreplay between two longtime lovers. In the third blink of an eye, he was aroused beyond all reason. Arousal mixed with the hot, humid air of the Argentinian jungle surrounding him, and the drumming rhythm of her untamed heartbeat against his own chest...

Now or never, that was all he could think. He did want it now, wanted her now. And she wanted him. There was no mistaking her intention in the way she pressed her pelvis hard into his erection and gyrated. There was no mistaking her intention when she broke their kiss, leaned her head back and looked into his eyes. This was everything the Pampas grass along the side of the road had promised to be, and more.

Now or never. There was no way in hell he was turning his back now. No way in hell he was turning his back on Amanda. So, in the fourth blink of an eye, Jack scooped her into his arms and carried her across the room. Definitely now, he thought as he laid her on the bed. But what about later? It was a thought that had no place between them, a thought he put away the instant her gauzy blouse came off. After that, Amanda consumed him in every way a man could be consumed, and he was a man who wanted to be consumed.

No regrets. No thoughts. Nothing but the moment they both wanted. Or the night. And once he looked down at the beautiful woman undressed and opening her arms to him, he knew a night would never be enough. Another hell to endure.

CHAPTER EIGHT

"NO WAY!" Jack exploded, wadding the test results and hurling them at the wall. "We're having the water filtered and boiled, so there's no way in hell the Giardia is getting in." Which should have been the case by all logical standards, except there'd been two new cases diagnosed in the past twelve hours, making the day go from one of the best in his life to one of the worst. From afterglow to aftershock. He was reeling from it, seething, angry. "So, we've got another source, and I don't even know where to start looking for it."

"It's not your fault, Jack, but if we don't get this thing figured out soon, we're going to be forced to close down temporarily." Ben ran a frustrated hand through his hair. "I can't keep putting my patients at risk. Giardiasis in itself is treatable and not life-threatening, but if someone else with an underlying condition comes down with it…"

Jack's thoughts instantly went to Renata. As of an hour ago she was still critical, still fighting for her life. Her doctors were optimistic, but optimism didn't fix the problem because Ben was right. There might be another Renata out there, one who wouldn't get the vote of optimism from her doctors. That wasn't acceptable. Neither was his failure to locate the source. "How long have I got?"

"Twenty-four hours at the most, if we don't have another case of it diagnosed. If we do, then we're shutting the doors immediately and sending the patients we have to any hospitals that have beds for them, which is going to make for one hell of a difficult transport. But that's all I can do. I'm already dismissing patients I'd like to keep around a little while longer, and closing down new admissions, except for dire emergencies. I've also postponed a couple of noncritical surgeries." He shrugged. "I should have gotten you here earlier, like Amanda wanted, before it all went to hell."

"She wanted me here earlier?" He was surprised yet pleased.

"I thought she was overreacting. Apparently I was underreacting. Either way, none of this is on you."

"Except the onus," Jack snapped, thoroughly irritated and not trying to hide it. "Look, I'm going to have to start again, so buy me time, Ben. Whatever it takes, buy me time." He shut his eyes, trying to visualize, trying to mentally see something he'd missed. All the usual water sources, anything with running water. All the unusual sources, anything with standing or accumulating water. He'd looked. Cultured every last one of them. So what was it? What the hell was it he was missing? "Did Amanda ever tell you what happened in Big Badger, Texas?" he asked, opening his eyes.

"You mean that E. coli epidemic?" Ben's eyes indicated he wasn't interested but was trying to be polite.

"Lots of people got sick, and I kept checking all the usual places and coming up empty."

Ben cocked his head, his attention a little more stirred now. "What's that got to do with Caridad?"

"Crazy thing. I found it in the least likely place…an innocent little jar of jam people were buying right and left from one of the locals. She was known for her strawberry jam and half the people in town bought from her. The same half who came down with E. coli."

"Strawberry jam?" Ben frowned, shook his head. "I'll be damned. Who would have ever thought…?"

"Exactly. Who would have ever thought? But she was using contaminated strawberries and made freezer jam, not the old-fashioned kind you jarred up in a water bath."

"So what might have been killed by the heat of the boiling wasn't."

"And I was looking for E. coli in all the wrong places…which in that case were the usual places. What I didn't take into consideration was that the least likely place was the most likely because the medium for growth was different."

"Which has what to do with our situation?" Ben asked. "Giardia doesn't have a myriad sources, like E. coli does."

"Don't know, but I'll get back to you with the answer in twenty-four hours or less," he said, on his way out the door. Then he stopped but didn't turn back to face Ben. "And when I give you your answers, I'm going to ask you a question to which I'll expect an answer. Last time I wasn't involved enough to be part of it. This time I am."

"I don't want to hurt her, Jack. That's not what any of this is about. I just want to protect her."

Finally, Jack turned back around. "I wanted to protect someone once. Someone I loved every bit as much as you love Amanda. So I understand what you're trying to do. But what I also understand is that she believes you know something she has a right to know. I think you do, too. What I also think is that it's not your right to keep it from her. She believes you're betraying her, Ben, and I agree with that, as well. You are."

Ben shut his eyes for a moment and rubbed his temples. "I heard you're going to the Pampas with her."

It wasn't a place he ever cared to see again, but for Amanda…anything. "Yes. Because she can't do this alone."

"You're right. She can't. But she's not going to listen to me if I tell her."

"Do you expect me to stop her? Is that what you're saying?"

"What I'm saying is that if you love her, you'll do what's right."

"Yet you love her, and you won't." He drew in a jagged breath, trying to fight back his anger. It wasn't a good situation, not for anyone, and he truly didn't blame Ben. But he didn't agree with him, either.

"Look, this isn't between you and me, and I don't want to make it that way. Okay? But I want to help Amanda find what she needs. Or be there to support her if she doesn't. Either way, she's made her decision to go and I've made mine to help her. I only hope you can live with what you've decided to do, because losing Amanda from your life…" Jack didn't finish the sentence because he'd thought it through to the end, to the worst possible scenario. Not having Amanda there in any way shook him to the very core.

"Can I help you, Doc K?" Ezequiel asked, running up to Jack as he simply stood in the hospital kitchen, staring at the sink, visualizing the slow drip coming from the faucet and the plumbing beyond that was hidden by the wall. "I can look at things good, just like you do."

Jack chuckled. The innocence of a child transcended cultures. Last night, with Amanda, the desire to be a father had hit Jack again.

It was the first time he'd felt it since Rosa's mother had delivered Rosa then died, leaving him with that precious little baby to care for. For a moment back then he'd had so many dreams, a lifetime of them for Rosa. One minute there had been no entanglements in his life, no plans for his own future other than doing more of what he was doing.

Then the next moment...those beautiful brown eyes, too young to even focus on him, yet with the way Rosa had looked up at him everything had changed in that instant. Everything he'd known about himself had suddenly been different because a child had been born, and she had become his.

But he'd thought ahead, to a child with Amanda. And he'd had to stop it. Stop the thought, stop the delusion and, more than anything, stop tempting himself with the notion he could have a future with her. The desire was there, but it took a hell of a lot more than desire to build a life, and he'd thrown out his building tools when Rosa had died because then, more than any other time in his disjointed life, he'd caught the clear vision of what he wasn't supposed to do.

Now he had last night to deal with. The best night of his life, but ultimately another delusion. "What I want you to do for me, Ezequiel, is take me on another tour of the hospital, of the surrounding buildings, of anything connected to the hospital. That way, we can look together." Suddenly, his thoughts shifted to the boy. What would happen to Ezequiel if the hospital closed? Would someone take him in or would he be shuffled into living on the street?

See, there he was, doing it again. Thinking about the things he couldn't have. Because he couldn't take Ezequiel home with him, and he couldn't stay here to take care of him. Why did he always do that? Why did he always go to these places he didn't belong? "Okay with you?"

"Okay with me," the boy said, giving Jack a thumbs-up sign.

"Good, then let me go..." Go and see how Amanda was doing? He'd left her at daybreak, when the promise of a new day had caused him to see what he was doing. She was vulnerable, depending too much on something that wouldn't come through for her. Because she expected, had the optimism to expect that life worked out. He didn't, because he already knew that life didn't work that way. Did she love him? Dear God, he hoped not. Did he love her? "Go grab some testing supplies, and I'll meet you in the storage shed outside the hospital."

Ezequiel scampered away to his task, leaving Jack *and* his quandary to stare out the window and figure out a way to focus harder. Or split himself in two.

"As they would say, a penny for your thoughts," Amanda said, stepping up behind Jack and slipping her arms around him.

He stiffened, not because of her closeness but because he loved the feel of her and she was already stirring him up again. "My thoughts? Giardia, and where it's sneaking in."

"Well, that sure was my penny's worth," she said, sounding surprised and stepping back.

"Look, I'm sorry. But Ben's on the verge of closing the hospital temporarily if I can't find it," he said, "and I'm on a deadline to figure it out."

"What?" she asked, her face draining of color. "Are you serious? He's going to close us?"

"He's already reducing services, and that's probably the best thing to do as I haven't found the real source. I mean, people are getting sick while

I'm…" He didn't finish the rest of it. Failure was failure, no matter who or what he failed. It was all the same, and the reasons didn't matter.

"I knew it wasn't cured. I should have spent the night…" He didn't say the word. It was hurtful, and he didn't want to be hurtful to her. "Look, I'm sorry. But I'm preoccupied. Frustrated. I need some space so I can just…"

"You've got your space, Jack." She took another step back. "There, space." And another step. "More space."

"Amanda, we started something I can't finish. I'm sorry, but that's how it is."

"I suppose you're right," she said, fighting to keep her composure. "That's how it is, and it's not like you didn't tell me. You did. Every step of the way. But you know what, Jack? While you may have your regrets over getting involved with me, I don't regret anything with you. You're an amazing man who just doesn't get what's amazing in himself."

"No regrets, Amanda. Not about you." He took a step toward her, reached out his hand to take hold of hers and pull her closer. But she wrenched back, like she'd touched her finger to a flame.

"Don't, Jack. Just…don't. We had our night. It's all I ever expected from you. Although I'll admit that I didn't expect to wake up alone. Guess I should have seen that coming, too, right?"

"I don't have time for this," he said, so torn between duty and Amanda his head was spinning. "But later. We'll talk later. Okay?"

She took another step back. "Look, I've got to go and make a maternity call, and Ezequiel's out there now, waiting for you."

He glanced out, clenched his jaw. "Later," he said again, regretting that he had to go. "And, Amanda, please, don't ever think I have any regrets." Confusion, though, was an entirely different matter because falling in love shouldn't be so damned difficult.

Amanda watched Jack from the kitchen window. Watched him walk across the hospital compound and meet up with Ezequiel at the shed. Jack's stride was angry, his physical comportment even angrier. But with himself? Or with her? Either way, it didn't matter anymore. He was everything he'd promised he'd be—a man who wouldn't stay. Too bad she hadn't listened to him before she'd fallen in love.

"You've got it that bad for him?" Ben asked, from across the room.

She didn't turn to face her brother. "Why would you care?"

"That's not fair, Amanda. I've always cared. You know that."

"Then tell me what I need to know," she whispered, so close to tears she wasn't sure she could hold them back. Yet she wouldn't let Ben see. Wouldn't let Jack see. Everything hurt, and she didn't know how to stop the pain. But she was Amanda Robinson. Strong, adopted kid. Good doctor. Totally devoted to the humanitarian causes. Yes, that was who she was, and that was who Ben saw when she finally turned around to face him.

"Clearly, you won't do it because you love me as a sister. I can deal with that. But you owe me,

Ben. I helped build this hospital with you, and I work myself to death to keep it funded. So, if you can't respect me as your sister, then respect me as your business partner. I have the right to know why we built this hospital in Argentina." She leveled a cold gaze on him. "Tell me, Ben. Or I'll get on a plane right now and go and ask Mother."

"You can't do that!" he warned.

"She's fragile, Ben. But her mind is clear. She knows the answer to my question."

"That's ugly of you, Amanda."

She shook her head. "Not ugly. Desperate. And tired of begging. Everybody I've ever loved has kept secrets about me. You don't know how that feels, and I can't even describe it. But it's like everything I've ever counted on has disappeared, and all I want to do is get it back."

"Then answer one simple question for me."

"What?"

"Do you love Jack Kenner?"

"What does that have to do with anything?"

"Because at the end of this, I want you to have someone, and I don't think it's going to be me."

"No," she choked, so close to tears again she didn't care now if Ben saw them fall. "I'll still have you, and Mother."

"Do you love him?"

She nodded. "Doesn't matter, though. Jack doesn't love me. I think he tried, or convinced himself he was trying. But I'm not sure he *can* love."

"Maybe he can love, but he can't accept it."

"And I'm not the one who can help him with that because I love him and he knows that, and it tortures him." She wrapped her arms around herself and sighed heavily. "Talk about all the worst possible elements for a relationship. Or, actually, there's nothing to talk about since there is no relationship."

Ben shook his head. "See it for what it is. Give yourself some space, some time, and I promise you, you'll see it for what it is. So now let me open another wound for you, because that's what I'm about to do. And I'm so sorry…"

"I can take it," she whispered, reaching out for Ben's hand.

He shook his head, refusing her gesture. Blinked back his own tears. Then steadied himself with a deep breath. "I don't know much about our parents' fascination for Argentina because, like you, I was told not to ask questions. Dad was a pretty exacting man when he wanted to be, and he loved Mother... I can't even begin to understand that kind of love. But it was so fierce, Amanda. Sometimes I'd see it just in the way they looked at each from other across the room. Or the way she'd simply lay her hand on his arm."

"When he talked too loud," Amanda said, smiling. "That was the signal."

"Then you saw it, too?"

She had but, unlike Ben, she believed she could understand a love like that. Or was just beginning to. "All the time."

"I only wish..."

"No regrets between us, Ben. We move forward from here. No matter what you're about to tell me, we move forward, together, from here. I promise."

"Don't give away your promises so quickly, Amanda. You may regret it."

Now she was scared. For herself. For Ben. For the memories she was afraid she was losing. And for Jack, who would be lost to her for reasons she couldn't change. "They lied, didn't they?" she asked, the words so jagged and sharp she could almost taste the blood on them. "Our parents lied to us, didn't they?"

Ben nodded. "I used to listen to them talk. Usually around us it was always about family things, school, work, you know, ordinary stuff. But after we went to bed at night they'd talk about earlier days in their marriage, when they…" He swallowed hard. "Amanda, our parents were volunteers for an organization that traveled around the world providing services, like teaching or physical labor, to impoverished areas. Dad taught agricultural techniques, Mom taught school. Young children, mostly."

"What? Why didn't they…? I don't understand." Growing up, the only thing she'd known about her parents' profession had been what she'd seen every day. They'd owned a ranch, raised sheep for the wool. Had been very successful at it.

"Neither did I. Not at first, anyway."

"Then how did you find out?"

"When they first brought you home, I was insecure. I thought they were going to trade me in. You know, replace me with you. Remember how I used to try and find ways to get rid of you?"

She nodded.

"Well, part of that involved spying. I used to listen to their conversations when they thought I was in bed. And I snooped through some of their personal belongings. It wasn't right and I knew that. But I did it anyway because I was just looking for something that would convince them to keep me." He grinned devilishly. "Or blackmail them into keeping me."

"And here I thought you were the perfect big brother."

He shrugged. "A kid's got to do what he's got to do. In my case, it worked out for a little while. I was gathering all kinds of information. One thing I discovered was that they lived in Argentina for two years. In fact, I'm pretty sure I was conceived in Argentina, because that's how the timeline worked out, according to some old pocket calendars I found. So that's probably the reason they returned to the States—to have me here. But who knows? Maybe I was actually born in Argentina, too. They lied about other things, so..."

He broke off his words. Swallowed hard. "See, that's what I didn't want you to know."

"That they lied?"

"If they lied, how do we know the truth about anything? Maybe I'm adopted, or... That's just it. How are we supposed to know *anything?*"

"And you've been carrying that around..."

"For years. When I was a kid, I didn't really understand it. But as I got older..." He shrugged.

"But Argentina. If they worked for a charitable organization here, it would have been a noble thing. Maybe they didn't lie so much as they didn't want to talk about it because that would make them seem like they were bragging or seeking some kind of praise or attention for it. Couldn't that have been it?"

Ben shook his head. "I kept asking them to tell me about when they lived in Argentina, and they ignored me every single time. So I went into the attic one night—"

"And found my birth records?" she interrupted, suddenly hopeful.

"No birth records. But I did find pictures, and clothes…fajas, ponchos, one particularly impressive rastras." An elaborate gaucho belt made with leather. "It was decorated with old coins, had a silver horse silhouette on it. I found a picture of Dad wearing it, along with full gaucho garb. He and Mother were at some kind of festival, dancing. And they looked so—so happy. Happy in a way I'd never seen them look. Anyway, that belt never made it back into the trunk. I kept it hidden, would sneak it to school with me and put it on. Dad showed up one day, unexpectedly, and caught me wearing it. So I told him what I'd found, that I'd seen all these pictures of them when they lived in Argentina.

"And he denied it, Amanda. Rather than ignoring me the way he usually did when I asked questions, he said they'd never lived here, never even been here. But I know what I saw—including their old passports, which clearly showed them coming to Argentina numerous times, even after I was born."

"I—I don't understand why they'd do that." Ben did, though. She could see it in him, some awful truth he was still holding back. Maybe this was the awful truth that cut him so deeply that what she was seeing was his own wound, the one that might never heal.

"That's what I've been asking myself for years. Never could figure it out so I gave up on it, because it's not easy going around telling yourself that your parents deliberately lied to you. Especially when we had such a good family. You know, close. So I gave up on thinking about it. But Argentina loomed over me like a big mystery and it turned into an obsession. Eventually, I started studying about it, trying to figure out what our parents were hiding. It made it better calling it a mystery rather than a lie, by the way."

"You never solved your mystery?"

"No. But the reason we built the hospital here is because I fell in love vicariously. Through my studies, Argentina became my passion. I knew the land, knew the people, became aware of the needs."

"And you never told me any of this? Why not, Ben? Maybe you didn't know I was from here, but why didn't you let me know what you'd found out?"

"Dad warned me, too, like he did you when you wanted to search for your records. Told me not to upset Mother. Then with her cancer…"

"What could we do?" she asked.

"All I ever meant to do was protect you from finding out they'd lied."

"But who protected you?" She ran to her brother and threw her arms around his neck. "I'm so sorry."

"Then we're good?" he asked.

"The way we always have been." And she felt better. Still, she sensed there was more. More information, more lies? Or simply more confusion? She didn't know. In fact, what Ben had revealed actually raised more questions and gave her no answers. Yet she had her brother back, and maybe that was the most she could hope for. "I'm still going to look," she warned as they headed out of the kitchen together. "I won't involve Mother in it, but it's my life and I have to keep searching."

"I never thought you'd do otherwise."

"But not with Jack. I have to do this alone. Have to find the strength in myself to do it, rather than relying on him to get me through. I think I was hoping for easy answers, and that relying on Jack would help me find them. He's a man of his word, and I know he wants to help me, but I need...me."

"Even if he loves you?"

She shook her head. "No. Because I love him. I've seen his choice even though he tries hard to hide it. So it's time I respect that, because I can't spend my life with a man who tries hard to love me but can't ever get there. I want to wake up in the mornings with someone I love, who loves me just as much. Make a home with him, have children with him, grow old with him." She brushed a tear from her cheek.

"Not with someone who's simply making the effort. It wouldn't be fair to me. Or to him. Jack may want to love me, but he can't. And maybe I should be able to figure out why but…but it hurts so bad. Which is why I have to go to the Pampas alone. I love him, can't have him, and I have to figure out how to reconcile myself to that." Swatting back another tear, she went on, "So, Ben, you owe me. And I expect you'll do this one thing for me."

"What?"

"Stall him. Don't let him know I've gone. Keep him occupied, send him off on a wild-goose chase if that's what you have to do. I need a head start. Twenty-four hours. That's all I'm asking."

"Then what?"

She shrugged.

"What if he comes after you?"

"Jack reads the subtleties, sees things no one can. He'll understand."

"In other words, you're walking away. Just turning your back on the man you love and walking away?"

"No. I'm letting him walk away. He'll never do it if we're together because above everything else

Jack honors his obligations and, in the end, that's what I am to him. So this gives him his out." Because she could never walk away from him. Yet she could never bear to see him stay.

An hour later, her duffel already packed, and Hector on his way to drive her to the landing strip, Amanda watched Jack immersing himself in his process. He was standing outside the storage shed, simply staring at it. He was frustrated. She could tell from the rigid way he stood—shoulders squared, fists clenching at his sides. Angry with himself for missing something. Berating himself, thinking about turning away from medicine.

"Any progress?" she called to him, fighting to maintain a steady voice. Certainly their paths would cross again. Maybe here in Argentina. Perhaps back in Texas. Before then there would be distance and separation and different perspectives. Next time she prayed she would be able to stand face-to-face with him without struggling with a lip that wanted to quiver, tears that wanted to fall. A heart that wanted to shatter.

So for now she was faking her bravery.

"I think my perspective is too narrow," he said, as she walked over to him. "I keep looking at this scenario in terms of regular water sources, but there's something else, something I'm missing."

She stepped up behind him, nearly leaning into him. Wanting to touch him so badly she ached, yet knowing she couldn't or it would hurt more than it already did. "Or maybe you're not missing it at all," she said. "Maybe it's right before your eyes and you're not seeing it because something's standing in the way."

"What are you talking about, Amanda?"

"You and me, Jack. Under these circumstances…it doesn't make any sense. Can't make any sense. Especially when you consider how we could have started this back in Texas, yet I don't think you ever looked at me as anything other than your nephew's doctor."

"I looked," he admitted, fighting visibly to keep himself reined in. "Every chance I got. And it wasn't my nephew's doctor I was seeing."

"Did you? Because I never saw it." And she would have loved seeing it.

"You in your prim and proper white lab coat, hair pulled back..." He paused, frowned. Mumbled, "Lab coat. *You in your lab coat!*"

She saw the figurative wheels start to turn. Knew she was totally shut out now. Something was going on with Jack. His eyes were closed, his breathing almost non-existent. The way he always was when he was solving it in his head. In spite of her confused feelings, it was so exciting watching him in this process that she literally started tingling from head to toe. Barely risked taking a breath herself for fear she would interrupt an important moment the way she'd interrupted his life.

So she waited, watched the process churning in him, saw his face in deep frown, saw that frown begin to dissipate, heard his breathing get deeper, saw his shoulders relax. Felt on pins and needles until, finally, he opened his eyes and smiled. "I know," he said. "I know where the Giardia is coming from."

Two words. *I know.* Words that meant everything, and nothing. For she knew, too, only not the source of the Giardia. "Tell me what you know," she whispered, knowing his next words wouldn't be the words she wanted most to hear.

"The bedsheets."

"The bedsheets?" she asked, once again caught up by his process. "I don't understand."

"You said the local women launder them, right?"

"But Giardia has to stay viable in a wet environment."

"Unless it encapsulates into a cyst. In other words, dries out and goes dormant."

"Then what would make it come back to life?"

"Maybe someone continually exhaling into the sheets." He smiled. "Just a guess, and it's off the charts as a standard explanation, but if you put cyst-contaminated sheets on every bed, chances are some of the cysts will become activated by someone breathing on them, then invade that person."

"What made you think of the sheets?"

He grinned. "You, in that lab coat. Mentally, I took it off you and you were naked underneath. Then we were in bed, and afterward you were snuggling into me, sleeping. You sleep on your side, Amanda."

"I know that." It was an image she didn't want in her head now. Didn't want any images of them together in her head, because those images and that reality hurt too badly.

"Your breath on me when you slept…warm, moist."

"Then what you're telling me is that I have breath to awaken the sleeping Giardia," she retorted, trying to keep that proverbial stiff upper lip. "Which means you've got work to do now."

"Work to do. Blessed, sweet work!" He picked her up, twirled her round and kissed her hard on the lips. "But we'll talk later, like I said," he said, setting her back down. "Because maybe we don't make sense, but neither does Giardia in the bedsheets."

Giardia in the bedsheets. She turned round and walked away in relief as Jack sprinted back to his makeshift lab. Stopping for a moment, she pressed her fingers to her lips, the taste of him still there. Then she braced herself and continued on to the Jeep, where Hector was awaiting her. Jack wouldn't see her crawl into the seat, wouldn't see them drive away. All he'd see would be the results of his efforts—the way it should be.

Different paths, she thought as they pulled away from Caridad, and she refused to look back. Different paths that couldn't converge. For a moment she'd thought they could. But she'd fooled herself.

CHAPTER NINE

"When did she leave?"

"Late yesterday. Oh, and in case you're interested, I was supposed to give her a twenty-four-hour head start before telling you."

"You should have told me right away. Before she had a chance to get on the plane. Or even leave the hospital."

"What would you have done if I had? Dropped everything, let the giardiasis go for another few days while you went after her?"

"I would have stopped her from going alone. Convinced her to wait another day or two."

"How, Jack? Tell me how, because this is Amanda we're talking about, and nothing's ever stopped her before."

"Okay, then. I'll go after her now."

"And do what? She went alone because she

wanted to go alone, so what is it you think you're going to change by going after her?"

"It's not about what I'm going to change. It's about what I'm going to do when her world changes all around her. She can't do this alone."

"I know that," Ben said. "Which is why I broke my promise and told you."

Jack shut his eyes, rubbed his forehead. "Look, have you got one more favor you can call in? I need a plane ride."

"I can get you a plane ride, but make sure this is what you want, because Amanda's going to push you away with everything she's got."

"Then I'll push back."

"I hope so, because…"

Jack watched the color literally drain from Ben's face, and everything he'd suspected was suddenly confirmed. "Damn it to hell, Ben. You know, don't you? You know what she's going to find if she keeps looking."

"What do I know? That my parents didn't adopt her? That they walked into one of the villages and just took her? I don't know that. How could I, when all they ever did was…?"

"Lie?" Everybody was doing it, coming in taking abandoned children like they were shopping in a grocery store. Thousands of children disappeared. The assumption was they were going to good homes, people desperate for children were circumventing adoption because it was easier. Still… "They lied to you, they lied to Amanda. And you let her go down there by herself?"

"I didn't let her go, Jack. She went. And I couldn't leave the hospital."

"And neither could I," he said. "Damn it! That's why she left when she did. Because nobody could go after her."

"With Amanda, that's what you get. She makes her opportunities. Oh, and she figures you'll take the hint that she wants to be left alone, or more likely that I'll tell you she wants you to leave her alone. She's giving it to you as your way out. But I think you'll get on the plane that will be waiting for you on the landing strip as soon as you can get there. And that's why I didn't go after her.

Because I would have, Jack. I swear to God, I wouldn't have let her do this by herself if I hadn't thought you'd be there to help her."

He wanted to be angry…at Ben, at Amanda, even at himself. But there was no point. Short of tying her up, he couldn't have stopped her. "Does she know what's happened to the children? Has she ever given you any indication that she's aware of any of that?"

"No. She doesn't know."

"You're sure?"

"You've never seen Amanda go after a worthy cause. If you think what you know in her now is stubborn and aggressive, you don't have a clue. If she believes, she believes with her whole heart. And if it's about children… Look, Jack. She adored our parents, and they doted on her, however they adopted or didn't adopt her. It's not going to be easy on her, accepting what they may have done, accepting that even after I'd promised her the truth, I gave her only half of it. And you… I'm not even going to tell you what's going on in her head about you. That's one for you to solve."

"So if I leave right now, you've got things under control here? Because if you don't, I can't go. You know that, don't you? As much as I want to go after Amanda, I won't if we're not squared away here."

Ben nodded. "We're good. Plenty of medical help. And now that we know Mrs. Ortiz was washing our sheets in a creek, trying to save money, we're going to let all the volunteers come here to do the laundry. In filtered water."

"For what it's worth, you protected your sister the way you should have, and you protected your parents as well by never saying anything. Not an easy thing to do because I know it's been tearing you up. But in your place I would have done the same thing. In the end, that's what it's about. We take care of the people we love." Something Ben had done far better than he had.

He blinked hard, trying not to think about Rosa. But she was always there, always reminding him. So now it was time to face up to it, face up to everything he'd done, everyone he'd failed, because this was about Amanda. Only Amanda.

* * *

Paso Alto, the homecoming he'd never wanted. Not thinking about it the whole way down here had been one way to avoid it, but now here it was, at the end of the dirt landing strip, waiting there for him the way it had been the first time he'd ever set foot in this village.

Except two years ago he'd come to cure a village illness. Malaria everywhere. People had been wary. He had been an outsider, not one of them. Not even close to being one of them, and he had never kidded himself about that. His life had been about traveling to these remote areas and dealing with issues, not people. But here he'd decided to stay and deal with the people.

The people…up ahead of him as he walked down the road to the center of the village, he saw them watching the plane taxi back out and take off. Had they changed? He had. And the hell of it was he wouldn't recognize faces. Not most of them, anyway. Or maybe he didn't want to recognize faces because what if he did? What would he do if he came face-to-face with one of the people who'd stolen his precious Rosa?

"Not easy coming back, is it?" Richard Hathaway asked. He was the only friend Jack had here, the only one who'd tried to help him find Rosa. And the one who'd stood next to him at Rosa's grave the day Jack's world had ended. "Wasn't sure I'd ever see you again."

"Wasn't sure I'd ever do this," Jack said, thrusting out his hand to shake Hathaway's then pulling the man into his embrace.

Richard Hathaway, a rotund septuagenarian with shocking white hair, ran the local orphanage and school. He'd come here thirty years before as a missionary, met the love of his life in another missionary and found his place. Lucky man.

"Well, it's a good thing. We all have our demons to face, don't we?

"Did Amanda find you?"

"She came to the orphanage last evening, asked to look through the records."

"And?"

"We took her in. Now she's still looking. Things

are in a bit of a mess, and I never was very good at the paperwork." He grinned. "Which may work out since I know exactly where your young lady is right now. She's with my *young* lady, enjoying lunch at the village fountain."

"After I phoned earlier, did you tell her I was coming?"

Richard shook his head. "Over the years I've had hundreds of people coming here, looking through my records. People just like your Amanda, trying to discover who they are, how or if they were adopted. They walk away heartbroken, because what most of them hope to find isn't out there. Most of the lost children were never recorded. And while I raise orphans and school them and give them a place to eat and sleep and be safe, I don't know what it's like to be out there alone, not knowing who you are. I can only observe it. But what I know is that Amanda needs the kind of support I can't give her. The best I can do for her, or for anyone like her, is give them a bed while they search, let my Martha cook them a few meals, grant them access to whatever I have and hope they discover what they need. So go and do what you have to then afterward you'll know where to find her."

"Do you know how difficult it is just to walk through town?"

"The most difficult step was getting off that plane. The rest will be easier."

He hoped so, because after he and Richard parted company farther up the road, the same nervousness returned to haunt him that he'd been feeling all the way down here. So it was one step at a time, past the marketplace and the little out-door café he'd stopped at nearly every day when he'd lived here that now he refused to remember. On down the road, past a family lumber mill and a bakery that pounded the best tortillas he'd ever eaten in his life, but refused to think about be-cause just beyond that was the office. His office. His little house next door.

At first he thought about crossing the road, pretending it wasn't there. But out of the corner of his eye he saw the window to the front bed-room. Tiny. Pink. Rosa's. The curtains were yellow-striped now, and the chair on the front porch where he used to sit and hold her had been replaced by a swing. Same house, though, and he couldn't refuse to acknowledge that because to do so would be to blot out the few memories he wanted to hold on to. Painful as they were, they were all he had.

However, he didn't stop. No, he continued on because he had to put away his past to help Amanda through her future. Because she could continue to look and, one way or another, he was determined to be at her side. He owed it to Rosa, the little lost child of his heart. But he also owed it to Amanda, who'd found her way into his heart when he'd thought there was no room for anyone other than his daughter. In her way, she was a lost child, too.

Jamming his hands into the pockets of his cargo pants, Jack held his head up, looked down the road to the church and the hill behind it that concealed the graveyard. It wasn't good. Not yet. But it would be. It *had* to be.

* * *

Amanda glanced down the road, blinked twice, took another look. "That's…" she started to say.

Martha Hathaway looked up from the bowl of fruit she'd been picking from, smiled and nodded. "As handsome as ever. I'm glad to see him return. He was an outstanding doctor, so good with the people here. A very generous, caring man. Always figured he would come back someday. Just didn't know what would make him do it."

"Why wouldn't he return?"

"When it's time, that's for the two of you to talk about. But I'm so glad he's here because Richard and I are quite fond of your young man, Amanda."

She glanced at Jack again, standing on the road. Not moving. And her heart lurched. She'd always seen that distance and sorrow in his eyes in those off-guard moments. It was what he tried to keep hidden behind his gruff facade but she observed the emotions the way he observed his bugs. And what she observed…what she knew now was that it was connected to this place. "He's not my young man," she said, still watching him. "Just a colleague."

"A colleague who causes you to stare off into space and sigh." Martha capped her bowl of fruit, patted Amanda on the hand and stood. "If you catch up to him, bring him round tonight. Argentina dinnertime. Tell him I'm going to make a lovely stew with sausages. He's partial to that, you know." She laughed. "Or maybe you didn't."

With that, seventy-year-old Martha Hathaway dashed away with the agility of someone half her age, leaving Amanda alone on the edge of the fountain, her attention still fixed on Jack. For the first few hours she'd been here she'd hoped he would follow her because she was so…uncertain. But then it got back to what she already knew, that Jack kept himself apart. Whatever his reason, he *was* that solitary man down the road. He kept himself to himself because that was what he chose to do and, no matter how strong her feelings for him were, loving Jack would turn into a lifetime of loneliness. Alone, in a love affair for two… She was only now beginning to understand the hopelessness.

Yet here he was, and while her intellect was telling her one thing, listing all the reasons she should avoid him, her heart hadn't caught up to her intellect because she still wanted to run to him. Yet she was afraid to go. But her betraying heart beat a little faster, refusing to let in the knowledge that she shouldn't do this, shouldn't go to him, shouldn't watch him.

Watch was what she did, though, while her intellect weighed the battle to keep her in place. Watched him walking by the café, the lumber mill, the bakery. Curious how he slowed down at the little house near the bakery, like he wanted to look at it yet didn't, or wouldn't. Or…couldn't.

Was he looking for her? Wouldn't he have gone to the orphanage first, if he was? It didn't make sense, especially seeing how hesitant he was, standing there alone. She could feel the struggle in him, even from so far away. See the physical manifestation of it crush him down in a way she didn't understand.

He was an outstanding doctor, so good with the people here. A very generous, caring man. That was what Martha had said, and those things were still true of him, but now they were buried too deeply for anyone to see. Yet there had been a time when they hadn't been. "Jack," she whispered, still watching. "What happened to you here?"

Suddenly she knew that what she was watching wasn't about him coming for her, looking for her as she'd thought he was doing. It was more. This had been where Jack's life had begun to stagger, where he'd pulled himself away from the world, away from medicine. His own personal hell to face, yet he'd come here for her.

Which meant he loved her. Jack Kenner loved her! He *could* love, and he'd proved it, walking through hellfire to find her. It was a realization that should have set her to tingling. Except there wasn't a thought in her head other than Jack. *He needed her.* She didn't know how, didn't know why, but none of that mattered. He needed her and now it was time for her to prove to Jack that she loved him.

* * *

The dreaded walk. He'd thought about this day for two years. Hoped and prayed he wouldn't have to trudge along this road again, see the same sights, be reminded every step of the way. Yet he'd always known that he would have come back someday. To say goodbye. To put a proper headstone on Rosa's grave. To forgive, even though that was the one thing he didn't want to do. Something he'd fought hard against every day for the past two years.

Now, though, he had a reason to move on and he wanted to. With all his heart he had to. But doing it meant forgiving. That was where he had to start otherwise he'd stay stuck in the same place— alone. Without Amanda.

Yet going back was the worst thing he'd ever had to do. So he kept his eyes down to keep from looking at the old white church looming ahead and the burial ground behind the little hill on the far side of it. Because he didn't want to look at the grave. Not again. He had to, though, because the last time he'd taken the road he'd been blinded by…by so many things. Grief, anger, loss. *Hatred.* All because of that tiny mound of dirt with the hastily made wooden cross that bore the name *Rosa.* Not even a last name, because no one in the village would give her what was rightfully hers. Just "Rosa," plain and simple.

On his last trip here he hadn't been able to say the things he'd wanted to say, which he'd regretted ever since. Because he wanted to tell Rosa how profoundly sorry he was for failing her. Tell her one last time how much he loved her. Beg God to let him trade places with his daughter. No, he hadn't said those things because too many people had watched, and yelled, and threatened to drag him out of town.

So, after two mired years, today was that day. He prayed he could find the strength to move on, for Amanda. It was what she needed from him, what he needed from himself. Not an easy thing, but it was time to put Rosa's memory in his heart where it belonged, time to move past the ugliness so he could hold on to the love. Put aside his heartbreak. Rosa deserved that. So did everyone he loved.

Then he would help Amanda through her heartbreak because when she learned the truth about who she was, her heart would surely break. And he would be the one to hold her.

"One minute at a time," he told himself, as he picked up his pace. That was all he could deal with. One minute, followed by another. He wasn't deluding himself into believing that those minutes would cure everything, but as he pushed open the creaking, rusty gate to the churchyard and headed round to the back, while his willingness waned, he could feel his conviction grow. "One minute at a time, one step at a time," he kept telling himself as he approached the tiny grave and came to a stop.

Odd, but no feelings rushed in the way he expected. No pain, no anguish. Just numbness. Was it because he'd fought so long to keep himself in a place where feeling nothing was easier? It had to be. He was still holding it all inside out of habit, afraid of what would happen when he let it go. Afraid to face the fact that his daughter was lying in that grave because he hadn't been able to save her.

His daughter…his flesh and blood. She should have been holding his hand now, tugging on it, looking up at him with beautiful brown eyes that clearly showed him she wanted to go and get ice cream, or play in the park, or find a puppy to adopt. That was the life he should have been living now. Not this empty existence where nothing mattered.

Because Rosa mattered. And Amanda… There was so much in his life that did still matter, and as he thought about it, thought about all the joy Rosa had given him in such a short time, and all the joy Amanda was giving him in spite of himself, that was when the emotion started to trickle back in. "Rosa," he said, dropping to his knees to run his fingers over her wooden marker. For the first time trying to remember, rather than trying to forget. Beautiful baby.

"I tried," he whispered, his voice breaking the words into shards. "But it wasn't enough…I wasn't enough." He could cure epidemics, diagnose the unknown, solve the impossible. Yet when it had come to Rosa... "I'm sorry," he said, swiping at the tears now sliding down his face. "So sorry."

"Sometimes it seems like we can never do enough," Amanda said, stepping up behind him. She stopped short, though, allowed him his distance. "We try, we give everything we have, and we fall short no matter what we do. And it hurts so badly we want to die. Then we blame ourselves for so many things...things we might deserve, things we don't deserve. And it consumes us, changes us, turns us into the kind of people we never thought we'd become. And the pain..."

She stepped forward and laid her hand on Jack's shoulder. "It doesn't go away. But it changes, and yet it won't let go."

"Sometimes living inside that pain is the easiest thing to do," he said.

"Until you find a reason to step outside it. Jack, when my father died, we'd been at odds for too long. I hurt him because all I could see was what I wanted to see, and he hurt me because he was trying to protect my mother. Neither of us deserved to have it end on such a dissonant note, yet it did. What you have to remember, though, is that love prevails. But not on its own. You have to let it prevail, otherwise it's just a word without meaning.

"Jack, I don't know what you're going through, don't know who Rosa was, but I love you and I want to help you face whatever you've got to face. You're not alone now."

"I don't remember a time in my life I wasn't alone. Except for those few weeks I had Rosa. And she made me realize how nice it is having someone to love, to take care of. I miss that. Miss her so badly there are days when I hope the sun doesn't come up so I can sleep through and discover that when I wake up tomorrow I'll realize it was all a nightmare." He turned to face her.

"Rosa was my daughter. I didn't want a child, never thought of myself in terms of being a father, yet there she was one day, in my life, in my heart…" He paused, reached out to touch the marker. "Her mother and I…it was…" He shrugged. "Brief. And we saw, early on, there was nothing…

So we ended. No hard feelings. I didn't know she was pregnant then one day I was called to go help the midwife with a difficult birth. And there was Carla, fighting to survive."

"But she didn't?" Amanda asked, stepping forward then sitting on the ground with him.

He shook his head. "The real fight was to save her baby. Then in Carla's last breath she told me the baby was mine. But she didn't have to tell me. I knew it the instant I held Rosa in my hands. There was this feeling… I can't describe it, but it was like everything in my life changed in the blink of an eye. Everything got better.

"Except it didn't because Carla had spent months lying to everybody she knew, including her family, about who Rosa's father was. Apparently she'd told them he was one of the locals, a love affair gone bad. Don't know why but I suppose it made life easier for her that way. Maybe less prejudice to face. Can't fault her for that since all I've been doing since then is taking the easiest way for me."

"So you were the only one who knew Rosa was yours?"

"The only one."

"Not even the midwife?"

Jack shook his head. "The thing is, at the time I didn't think it would be a problem. I'd planned on taking Rosa home with me and we'd have a life together. Stupid, simplistic dream."

"What happened?"

"She was ill. Had a congenital heart defect that started showing in her pretty quickly. But there was no place around here with the means to perform the surgery she needed. It should have been an easy problem to solve—take my daughter back to the States for surgery. I'd made the arrangements with a buddy from med school, and I was on my way to the airport, but…they stopped me."

"Who?"

"The town. They literally stopped me on my way to the taxi and took her away from me."

Amanda gasped. "How could they? I mean, didn't they know who you were? Maybe not as Rosa's father but as the doctor?"

"A lot of the people knew me, most of them trusted me, I think. I'd come down to chase after

malaria, decided to stay for a while because..."
He shrugged. "They needed a doctor, I suppose.
The thing is, even the people I treated turned on
me." He shut his eyes. "They took her, and hid her.
Shuffled her from house to house, family to family, village to village so I couldn't find her. But I
looked. Everywhere. Kept looking, kept knocking on doors. Then after weeks of it I suppose
Rosa's frail little body couldn't take it any longer
because I received a hand-delivered note from the
village priest telling me that her funeral service
would take place that very afternoon." He swallowed hard. "I wasn't allowed in the graveyard
until after she was buried."

Amanda gasped. "I'm so sorry, Jack. I can't
even begin to imagine..."

"I know they were trying to protect her, but I
kept telling them I was her father, and they didn't
believe me because too many people had taken too
many children, and to the people trying to protect Rosa I simply looked like one of the many.
Because of that she died, Amanda. I loved that
baby, and she died, and there wasn't a damn thing

I could do about it." He swallowed hard. "And no-body can understand what it feels like, knowing you failed your child in the worst way any parent could ever fail their child."

Amanda scooted closer to Jack and put her arms around him. For her support, for his, there wasn't a distinction now as the grief settled down over both of them. But finally she broke that silence. "Why, Jack? Who was taking the children? I don't understand."

Jack braced himself for this. It was time. Time for things to end, time for things to begin. Doing it here with Rosa was right because, like Amanda, she was part of the cycle of sadness that had touched and broken too many lives. So he shifted, took Amanda's hand and held on for dear life because nothing would be the same again, not for either of them. "First, just let me say I don't want to hurt you with any of this."

"What do you mean?"

"I didn't want to come back here. Not ever. Didn't want to face what they'd done. Most of all didn't want to face myself because living in my own little isolated world was what I deserved. Or believed I deserved. Then I met this wild, crazy woman who kept trying to turn my world upside down, and it's damn hard to stand firm when she's feeding you blueberries and stringing your bed with Christmas lights."

"This doesn't have anything to do with Rosa, does it?"

He was surprised her face was the picture of calm considering what he knew *she knew* was coming, but it was. Beautiful, serene face. "It has everything to do Rosa, and Ezequiel, and you, I think."

"Then tell me, Jack. Tell me what I believe Ben knows and you suspect. And how it all connects to your daughter, and to Ezequiel. And to me."

If only there was a way to shade her from this like the leaves of the massive ombu tree overhead shaded them. But there wasn't. She was sitting there, looking so brave and determined, yet he saw the uncertainty in her eyes. And here he was, faced with the moment, dreading it and hoping, at the same time, there was merit in the old adage that the truth would set you free. Still, all he could see in this truth was pain.

But it was time to quit protecting Amanda. She needed more. Returning to Paso Alto had been his starting place. Now it was time to give Amanda the same thing—her own starting place.

So he drew in a deep breath and began. "All the years I've traveled, I've seen so many orphaned children. Everywhere. Internationally, it's believed there are about one-hundred and forty-three million. In South America alone close to eight million. It's sad, Amanda. I've seen them everywhere and wondered why all the people who want children can't just go to these places and find them. Cut through the red tape. Give the children a home. You can't even begin to imagine…" He sighed.

"Happily ever after for everyone. In so many ways it makes sense. But there are laws and procedures that have to be in place so these children aren't exploited, and I understand that because they have to be protected above everything else. Unfortunately, the laws are broken anyway. Children have been taken without going through the proper procedures. Sometimes they're literally abducted. Picked up off the streets and carried away.

"The people who live here have seen that happen over and over, lived with it, watched the children being…stolen. That's why they stopped me. They didn't know I was Rosa's father and to them, doctor or not, I was just another one of the outsiders who had merely wandered in to take a child."

Amanda looked at Jack and the color from her face drained away. But she didn't ask. So he continued before the full realization of what he was telling her sank in. "I think, or I hope that most of the time the people who took these children did so with the best intentions. But the sentiment became *See an abandoned child, save the child.* Still is in some areas. I know that sentiment, understand it probably better than I understand almost anything else because all I wanted to do was save Rosa, and she wasn't an abandoned child. Even Ezequiel—my gut reaction to him was to take him home with me when I go because nobody will notice. So I know how so many of these people felt when they came here, or any number of other places, and saw these abandoned children literally up for grabs.

"Yet taking a child without doing it the proper way is wrong, and in some cases children who weren't orphaned were even taken. See an abandoned child, save the child, but don't bother to see if the child is really abandoned or part of a family. In the rush to grab *free* children, mothers and fathers lost their sons and daughters, and there's nothing right about that, no matter what the intention."

He brushed her cheek. "Children in South America were especially desirable...beautiful skin, beautiful eyes. There were so many orphans here, and since so much of the land was still rural the assumption was that in many of the areas no one cared. Or noticed."

Her breathing turned ragged as she struggled with the next words. "Is that me, Jack? Was I one of the children who was taken?"

"I'm so sorry, Amanda, but I believe you could

have been," he said, his voice barely above a whisper.

"And Ben? Does he know about these children? Does he think that I was…?"

Jack nodded. "That's something the two of you will have to work out, but he's devastated by this, devastated by the feelings he has for your parents and what they might have done."

"Yet he never told me."

"Because he was trying to protect you. And trying to protect your parents, as well."

"But they loved me, Jack. I know they loved me. So how could they…?" She shut her eyes, shook her head. "So how could they tell me the truth if they stole me? Yet how could they *not* tell me the truth if they didn't?"

"We don't know yet if it *is* the truth. There were many legitimate adoptions going on as well, especially in the early years. And now. So maybe the records really weren't kept, or your records got lost. Your parents were humanitarian workers here…"

"Who lied to me. Who would have had easy access to an orphan child. Which would make them part of the reason you weren't allowed to leave with Rosa. Because of what my parents did." She paused, and in a flash the pain on her face turned to pure, raw anger. "Jack, I…I don't know what to say. I can't even…" She paused again, shut her eyes, then pulled away from him. "You knew this, didn't you? You knew this all along."

"I suspected. Once I understood the confusion behind your adoption, I knew that could be the case. That your parents might have come here and taken you. Then when I found out how they'd lied…"

"Rosa was Mapuche. That day when you said you loved someone who was Mapuche… That's why you can't love me. How could you? My parents, what they did… And Rosa. I thought it was you, Jack. All this time, when you've pulled away or distanced yourself, I thought it was you. But it was…"

"Me," he said gently. "But not because I couldn't love you, Amanda. I have. I do. But I've been filled with so much hate and anger there wasn't room for anything else. Michael got in first, though. Just knocked right through it all and found a little place. Then you, and Ezequiel. But you all deserve more than a little place in my heart, and I couldn't let go of all my emotions to give you what you needed. When you left, when you came here alone, I knew what you'd be facing sooner or later, knew you shouldn't have to face it alone. But to be what you needed I had to get past all this."

"It can't work now. Don't you understand? My parents were part of your suffering, and every time you look at me you may want to love me, think you do love me, but what I came from will always be a reminder of what happened to your daughter."

"I've known that from the day I arrived in Argentina and you twisted my arm into telling you that you're Mapuche. And it hasn't changed the way I feel about you. But that's something you're going to have to trust, and I think you will when you're past the initial shock.

"The thing is, Rosa died because people cared about her. I've known that all along, but didn't want to see it. I knew the people here didn't want to harm her. And if your parents did simply take you, it's because they cared, too. What I want to believe is that they saw a beautiful child who needed a home, and loved her the way every child deserves to be loved."

"And you can just accept that, and move on?"

"Not alone. My daughter died, Amanda, and I'm still grieving. Still struggling with how I feel. Maybe I'm only just beginning to grieve the way I need to. But I can't do that by myself because I'll go right back to being myself—that grumpy recluse you met back in Texas. The one who finds it easier to stay numb."

"Always on the verge of quitting medicine," she added.

"Not medicine. I've never truly been on the verge of quitting medicine. More like on the verge of quitting me. I don't want to keep living with the pain, but being a doctor who failed to save his daughter is a pain that just keeps beating me down. Until you, I never had a reason to want to get back up again. To need to get back up."

"But you didn't fail her, Jack. The failure came from something you couldn't control. For Rosa, you were a perfect father who would have given his life to save his daughter. There's no failure in that. Only sadness for a little girl who didn't get to see how very loved she was."

"I want to stay here," he said. "In Argentina, at Caridad. Maybe come back here from time to time to put flowers on her grave and do some doctoring at the orphanage. But I don't want to stay here without you, Amanda. I don't want to be alone anymore."

"I keep thinking back to the first time I ever saw you…standing there in my office doorway, demanding my references."

He chuckled. "I remember that man. Pretty surly, wasn't he?"

"Surly, maybe. But I also saw the way you looked at your nephew later that day, at the hospital. You'd never even met him, yet that first look at him…"

"You saw that?"

"I saw everything." She blinked back tears.

"And knew everything I needed to know about you. That's why it hurt so bad when I didn't think you could love me, because that was the man I fell in love with. Maybe not at first sight. But at second sight, when I saw you with Ezequiel. And third sight, with Renata, and fourth with Alfonso… Everything I saw was someone you didn't see, or couldn't see, but I never, ever couldn't see that man. And he's the man I want to see every day, for the rest of my life."

"I'm still going to be grumpy sometimes. Can you put up with that?"

"And I'm still going to get obsessed with trying to find out who I am. Can you put up with that?"

"I'll have to go when there's an outbreak of some sort."

"And I'll be going back to Texas a couple times a month to check on some of my patients."

"But I won't be eating blueberries again."

"No blueberries?"

"Allergic. They really do make me break out in hives."

She leaned her head on his shoulder. "Yet you ate one for me."

"Because you were cramming it down my throat."

"Because you were being grumpy."

"Because you were making me happy."

Sighing, Amanda reached over and brushed her fingers across Rosa's marker. Then smiled. "It's better together. Whatever it is, whatever we've got to face, wherever we have to go, it's better together."

"I guess I've never had a Christmas without a Christmas tree, but this works," Jack said, grinning as he studied the outline of a Christmas tree Ezequiel had formed with strings of Christmas lights on the wall. It was rather amazing, actually. Quite ingenious. Made Jack wonder what kind of talents he would discover in his soon-to-be son. One perfectly good kid in need of parents, two not-so-perfect parents in need of a kid. It was a great way to start a new life—as a family of three.

Ezequiel grinned from ear to ear. "And there are

presents," he squealed, pointing to the wrapped packages sitting on the floor underneath the pseudo-tree. "Look at them! There are so many."

"All of them for you," Jack said, smiling. He'd avoided Christmas for years. Too much sentiment, too many memories. Yet today what he had was a life full of expectations. New things, good things. Journeys with Amanda as she went to look for her heritage. A son. The occasional call out to hunt down and take care of an epidemic. A home to build in Argentina, a hospital to help once he endowed some expansions, including a bigger office for Ben—although he was partial to the idea of taking over Ben's former office with its cramped space just because he had fond memories of being cramped in there with Amanda. Just the beginning of so many memories to come. "Except a couple for Amanda."

"Maybe one for Jack," she said, looking particularly pleased with herself.

They hadn't told Ezequiel their plan yet, but his adoption was in the works. It was going to be tricky because neither Jack nor Amanda were Argentinian citizens. But a strong recommendation from Richard Hathaway went a long way. So did a letter from the Paso Alto priest. The official assigned to Ezequiel's welfare was also optimistic. In fact, she'd promised her support. So it was all looking good.

"And me?" Ben asked, winking at Ezequiel. "Is there anything under that tree for me?"

"Your Christmas gift," Amanda told him, "is a holiday. You haven't been out of this hospital in ages, and considering all the stress you've just been through you need it. So Jack and I are going to take over for two weeks while you go someplace else and do whatever you want." She plucked an envelope from amongst the wrapped packages and held it up. "I know you've always wanted to see Tuscany, so this ticket will take you to Italy. Or you can exchange it for anywhere else you want to go."

Jack held up an envelope of his own. "And these two tickets will take us back home so I can take care of my personal effects and buy you a proper engagement ring, then maybe go and talk to your mother, if you're up to it."

Amanda glanced at her brother. "Maybe she'll tell me what I want to know, maybe she won't. I'm not going to press her for answers. But she has to know that, whatever she did, I love her and I forgive her. When I was in Paso Alto I saw too much guilt, too much pain, and it occurred to me our mother has lived with it herself all these years because of what I think she and Dad did. Just the way you've lived with the guilt, trying to protect me from it. So I have to let her know that, no matter what it was, I do love her.

"And I love you, too, Ben, for being the best big brother a girl could have." She reached out and took Ben's hand. "I'll be gentle with her. I promise."

"I know you will," Ben said.

"And two more presents, one from me and one not from me." Jack looked at Amanda. "Both for you."

"I love presents," she said, nudging Ezequiel to start unwrapping. So far, he was so caught up in simply looking at the presents, but at the prompt wrapping paper started to fly. And for the next half hour Amanda and Jack enjoyed everything about their first Christmas with their son.

"Now Christmas for us," Jack finally said to Amanda. "And your first gift comes from Father Garcia."

"The priest in Paso Alto?"

Jack nodded. "I never told you, but he was the one who literally took Rosa from my arms. His convictions were strong that he was doing the right thing, but since she died he's never been able to forgive himself. So I talked to him that day, after we left the grave. It's where I had to start to make things right again. Start to forgive. And he was so…sad, and so appreciative that I would stop to see him after what he'd done. Anyway, he's promised to help you by making contact with every priest he knows in the Pampas areas and ask them to search their records for any that might be yours."

She leaned over and gave him a proper kiss on the cheek. "Thank you for what you did for the father. You did a good thing, Jack. A very good thing, helping him get past it."

"Well, I hope this next present gets me a kiss on the lips."

"But I don't see anything else under the tree."

"Too big to wrap. Except the computer, which will be delivered in a couple of weeks."

"You bought me a computer?" she asked, smiling, but slightly puzzled. "Because we have a computer here."

"A hospital computer. But I'm having this one installed with software being designed especially for you and the foundation I'm endowing. Something we're going to run together with the help of Richard and Martha. Even Father Garcia."

"A foundation?"

He nodded. "That day in Paso Alto when Richard told me how many people like you show up at his orphanage, looking for records, I started thinking about how we could help their search."

Amanda's eyes widened, but she didn't say anything.

"We can do it from here, and from Paso Alto.

Transfer existing records to a searchable database. Search other databases for whatever we can find. It's not the perfect solution, but it's a start."

"I…I don't know what to say, Jack. I'm…"

"Speechless?" he asked, laughing. "Does that mean I'm finally going to get the last word?"

"And I'm going to learn the computer," Ezequiel said, grinning.

She looked at him, fighting back a laugh. "You knew about this, and you kept it a secret from me?"

"Doc K promised me a video game. I don't know what that is yet, but I think it's good. So I had to keep it a secret."

Amanda got up on her hands and knees and crawled over to Ezequiel, who was sitting in the middle of all his presents. Then hugged him. "It's very good," she said. "Everything is very good.

"Do I get any of that?" Jack asked.

She crooked her finger to beckon him over, and just as he leaned in for what he expected to be a kiss, she stopped him. "Thank you for doing that, Jack. It's important. It's something that can make a real difference. And it's worth more than a kiss," she said. "To help people find themselves…it's worth everything." Taking his hand, she placed it on her belly. "It's still early, just barely begun, but by next Christmas we'll be a family of four. My gift to you."

Speechless, he simply stared at her belly for a moment then stared into her eyes. "We did that?"

She nodded. "We did that."

Smiling, he pulled her into his arms, brushed a tender kiss to her lips then leaned down, pulled up her shirt and kissed her belly. After that he raised up and whispered, "Everything."

* * * * *

Mills & Boon® Large Print Medical

May

MAYBE THIS CHRISTMAS…?	Alison Roberts
A DOCTOR, A FLING & A WEDDING RING	Fiona McArthur
DR CHANDLER'S SLEEPING BEAUTY	Melanie Milburne
HER CHRISTMAS EVE DIAMOND	Scarlet Wilson
NEWBORN BABY FOR CHRISTMAS	Fiona Lowe
THE WAR HERO'S LOCKED-AWAY HEART	Louisa George

June

FROM CHRISTMAS TO ETERNITY	Caroline Anderson
HER LITTLE SPANISH SECRET	Laura Iding
CHRISTMAS WITH DR DELICIOUS	Sue MacKay
ONE NIGHT THAT CHANGED EVERYTHING	Tina Beckett
CHRISTMAS WHERE SHE BELONGS	Meredith Webber
HIS BRIDE IN PARADISE	Joanna Neil

July

THE SURGEON'S DOORSTEP BABY	Marion Lennox
DARE SHE DREAM OF FOREVER?	Lucy Clark
CRAVING HER SOLDIER'S TOUCH	Wendy S. Marcus
SECRETS OF A SHY SOCIALITE	Wendy S. Marcus
BREAKING THE PLAYBOY'S RULES	Emily Forbes
HOT-SHOT DOC COMES TO TOWN	Susan Carlisle

Mills & Boon® Large Print Medical

August

THE BROODING DOC'S REDEMPTION	Kate Hardy
AN INESCAPABLE TEMPTATION	Scarlet Wilson
REVEALING THE REAL DR ROBINSON	Dianne Drake
THE REBEL AND MISS JONES	Annie Claydon
THE SON THAT CHANGED HIS LIFE	Jennifer Taylor
SWALLOWBROOK'S WEDDING OF THE YEAR	Abigail Gordon

September

NYC ANGELS: REDEEMING THE PLAYBOY	Carol Marinelli
NYC ANGELS: HEIRESS'S BABY SCANDAL	Janice Lynn
ST PIRAN'S: THE WEDDING!	Alison Roberts
SYDNEY HARBOUR HOSPITAL: EVIE'S BOMBSHELL	Amy Andrews
THE PRINCE WHO CHARMED HER	Fiona McArthur
HIS HIDDEN AMERICAN BEAUTY	Connie Cox

October

NYC ANGELS: UNMASKING DR SERIOUS	Laura Iding
NYC ANGELS: THE WALLFLOWER'S SECRET	Susan Carlisle
CINDERELLA OF HARLEY STREET	Anne Fraser
YOU, ME AND A FAMILY	Sue MacKay
THEIR MOST FORBIDDEN FLING	Melanie Milburne
THE LAST DOCTOR SHE SHOULD EVER DATE	Louisa George